CW00394330

Copyright

This is a work of fiction. Names,
either the product of the author'
With the exception of well-known historical figures and places, any
resemblance to actual persons, living or dead, business
establishments, events or locales is entirely coincidental.

No part of this book may be reproduced in any form or by any
electronic or mechanical means, now known or hereafter invented,
including information storage and retrieval systems, without written
permission from the applicable author, except for the use of brief
quotations in a critical article or book review.

Any use of this work for machine learning or artificial intelligence
training purposes is expressly prohibited.

Copyright © 2019 (an early version of this story was first published in
2018)

Stock Photography by Period Images

Cover Design by Victoria Cooper

The purpose of copyright is to encourage writers and artists to
produce the creative works that enrich our culture.

The scanning, uploading, or distribution of this book without explicit
written permission is theft of intellectual property. Thank you for
your support.

This work was made possible by special permission through the de Wolfe
Pack Connected World publishing program and Dragonblade Publishing, Inc.
dba WolfeBane Publishing. All characters, scenes, events, plots and related
elements appearing in the original World of de Wolfe Pack connected series
by Kathryn Le Veque Novels, Inc. remains the exclusive copyrighted and/or
trademarked property of Kathryn Le Veque Novels, Inc., or the affiliates or
licensors.

All characters created by the author of this novel remain the copyrighted
property of the author.

Discover Kathryn Le Veque's de Wolfe series on Amazon

CONTENTS

On the wild heathlands of Dartmoor, the winds are howling and the mist is creeping over the dark crags, but Mallon and Geneviève's story awaits to warm your heart.

My heroines battle many of the same challenges we do today—striving for independence and self-determination, while yearning for true love.

Like the women (and men) in these tales, you're stronger than you may realize, more resourceful and more determined.

As for happy endings, we all need to believe that things can get better if we persevere, that there is hope, and the chance to embrace a life of love and friendship and contentment.

with warmest wishes to you

MASTER OF THE MOOR

BY EMMANUELLE DE MAUPASSANT

CAST

Lord Alfred de Wolfe – 8th Viscount Wulverton
Lord Mallon de Wolfe – 9th Viscount Wulverton
Lord Edward de Wolfe – younger brother to Mallon
Lord Hugo de Wolfe– Edward's son, and Mallon's heir
Lady Marguerite de Wolfe – mother to Hugo, and sister to Maxim

Muffin and Tootle – Hugo's Wolfhounds

Geneviève (Comtesse Rosseline) – widow to Comte Maxim Rosseline
Lisette – maid to Geneviève

Reverend Wapshot and Mrs. Griselda Wapshot
Beatrice Wapshot – their daughter

Dr. Samuel Hissop and Mrs. Violet Hissop

Lord Slagsby – Hugo's schoolfriend

Wulverton Hall staff

Mrs. Fuddleby – cook and housekeeper

Ida – the kitchen maid

Betsy – the parlour maid

Joseph Withers – the ancient butler

Silas Withers – Joseph's brother (former head
stableman)

Scroggins – the head stableman

CHAPTER ONE

Marseille, Late November, 1903

Lord Mallon de Wolfe, Viscount Wulverton, drew out his hipflask and called to the driver to get a blasted move on. He'd been fortunate in finding a cab waiting at the Marseille dock, and had promised double fare if they reached the train station before ten o'clock. Mallon had a first-class sleeping compartment booked and intended to make good use of it.

It had been a damnable day, a damnable week, and a damnable journey. With no berths available on the only passenger liner departing Constantinople, he'd been obliged to join a cargo ship. Not that he'd cared about the lack of comforts—nor the stench of sweat and latrines—but the confounded vessel had barely been seaworthy.

They'd crossed the Sea of Marmara, past the Greek islands and the toe of Italy, before the water sloshing onto the lower deck required all hands—his included—

to take shifts at the bilge pump. They might have diverted to Corsica for repairs, but he'd insisted they press on. Between them, their crew had been capable of keeping the boat afloat, and he'd been eager to press on. A few more days delay on top of twenty-three years might have seemed irrelevant, but Mallon was a man of sudden moods, and his mind was set upon reaching the country he'd left so long ago.

In some respects, he'd welcomed the physical effort, rather enjoying rolling up his shirt-sleeves. He had a great deal more brawn than most men of his age, thanks to his soldiering days and his fondness for pugilism. Nothing eased the temper like a few heated rounds in the ring.

Before long, he'd dispensed with his shirt altogether and applied himself like the rest, taking turns perspiring in that furnace-of-an-engine room to keep the dratted boat from sinking them to Neptune's embrace.

The journey had reminded him of his army days, when he'd been hunkered around the mess table, sharing whoever's cigarettes were dry, and eating sausages hot from the pan, paired with the standard ration of dry biscuit and a tot of rum.

Not that he indulged in nostalgia. After all those years serving with Her Majesty's Kabul-Kandahar Field Force, he had nothing to show for it but a shoulder that ached every day! They'd gotten most of the shrapnel out, but something remained—a souvenir as unwanted as the memories that went with it.

Much good it had done him to be mentioned in dispatches for 'outstanding courage under fire'. The accolade didn't bring back those who'd fallen beside him. He'd watched men's bones shatter and watched them bleed and die. As for bravery, he'd done nothing more than keep himself alive—and others as best he could.

Mallon swigged down the last of his flask, wincing as the harsh aniseed of the arrack hit the back of his throat. It was one thing they hadn't been short of on the boat—among two hundred cases of the stuff, no one had missed a few bottles.

He rested his head against the coolness of the window, watching the passing street lamps as the coach clattered up the rise of the Boulevard Voltaire. So much time had passed since he'd walked away from his legacy, and the past ten had been a shabby excuse for a life. It had been hard at times, in Constantinople, but the city offered anonymity. There, he was no one and nothing, and it was easy to find oblivion in the opium rooms, seeking escape from his regret and anger.

Now, all that was going to change. He was going to change. His father's death had seen to that. News of his passing, like that of his brother Edward over two years before, had come too late for Mallon to attend any funerals. He might have returned sooner, to pay his respects at Edward's grave, but his pride had stopped him from making the journey.

The wounds of his estrangement from his father remained raw but, despite the moor's tormenting associations, it was his home. He'd commitments to fulfil and wrongs to put right. How could he live with himself if he refused to face those challenges?

He was a de Wolfe, after all. Like his ancestors, he'd experienced the hell of the battlefield. He'd stared down death to serve his queen and his country.

With his father gone, the only demons left to face were those lurking within himself. Mallon wished to make himself anew, like moorland gorse awakening after winter's long frost. Perhaps he was fooling himself, but the pull of the place to which he truly belonged was too strong to ignore.

As for mourning his father, Mallon's grief was tinged strongly with resentment. The late viscount had never been the same after losing his wife—had retreated into his anguish too deeply to see that his sons needed their father's love. They had needed it more than ever after their mother's death. Edward had been a mere babe in arms, too young to be aware of much, but Mallon had known from the outset that something was wrong.

His mother had been perfectly well just the day before. Afterward, all trace of her vanished. Within a few days, every piece of the viscountess's clothing had been removed from the house. It was as if she'd never been. When Mallon had attempted to speak to his father of her, it had elicited the sternest of reprimands.

And then, Mallon had heard the servants' whispers.

She'd had a lover and ran away. At first, Mallon's heart had surged with hope. If she'd gone away, then she might come back. It had been a mistake to leave him behind.

Except that she couldn't return. She'd meant to start

a new life, far from Wulverton Hall, but had reached no further than the deadly mire, just below Fox Tor.

The man who'd waited for her had raised the alarm, but they'd never found her body.

Mallon hadn't been allowed to attend the burial, but he'd watched from one of the upper windows of the hall. The coffin was taken on a simple cart to the chapel, with only the priest in attendance. A coffin that was empty. His father had, at least, permitted a headstone, tucked in the far corner of the graveyard.

Mallon's mother hadn't loved him enough to stay. His father had barely known how to love at all. Mallon couldn't remember the viscount showing any physical affection for him, nor for Edward. He'd rarely tolerated having them in the same room. That pain lingered, whatever distraction he attempted.

As soon as he'd been able, he'd sought to escape, making his life far from the moor and those anguished memories. He'd sought a new home with the army, following in the footsteps of his all-revered ancestors. And he'd succeeded in finding some measure of peace—at least for a while.

"*Nous sommes ici, Monsieur!*" The driver pulled the horses to a standstill and jumped down. There was no baggage to bother with, Mallon having brought only a travelling portmanteau he could carry easily himself. It was just as well, since the train departed in twenty minutes and the ticket still needed collecting.

Stuffing the promised francs into the Frenchman's hand, Mallon made for the grand archway of La Gare de Marseille Saint Charles.

IT WAS TAKING all Mallon's self-control not to punch the conductor full on the nose.

"*Regarde mon billet!*" It was the fifth time he'd demanded that the man look at his ticket. Twice in French and three times in English, embellished with increasingly violent oaths.

"*Je ne peux pas vous aider, Monsieur.*" The conductor shrugged his shoulders. "*Vous devrez partir.*"

It was bloody hopeless! He was going to end up sleeping in the corridor at this rate and all because some damned idiot in the ticket office had managed to double-book his compartment, giving it to some other passenger entirely.

The bulb inside flickered, emitting a low buzz, offering barely enough light for him to see the occupant. Her abundance of skirts indicated a woman, but her veil prevented him from discerning more.

His final volley of expletives having caused the conductor to scurry away, Mallon placed his head in his hands. He was too tired for this. His only hope was to find space in the buffet car. If he gave the last of his ready cash to the *serveurs*, they might overlook him lying down on the seats there.

He took a final, yearning look at the compartment. Plenty of room and the bedding neatly stacked. Propriety would never permit them to share, but he wondered if the woman might consider lending him one of her pillows.

He was reluctant to ask. Though he'd managed to

wash before disembarking the ship, Mallon hadn't shaved in several days and his hair was long overdue a cut. The sight of him, not to mention his aggressive behavior, would hardly have created a good impression. Mumbling his apologies, he turned to leave.

"*Arrêtez, Monsieur*." She beckoned him to enter.

Mallon didn't need to be asked twice. Taking the banquette opposite, he leaned back against the velvet cushioning. With all the rushing about and his ridiculous labours on the ship, his shoulder was irking him.

He eyed the pillows again, wondering if he might beg one after all. "*Vous voyagez seul, Madame?*"

To his relief, she responded in his own tongue. "Yes, but with my maid. She has a compartment further down."

Mallon perked up a little. "I don't suppose…" He hated begging favors but had no wish for another sleepless night, snatching what rest he could elsewhere on the busy train. "Might she share with you, and I'll take her cabin? I can write a draft on my bank to compensate for your trouble—double the original cost, of course."

She seemed amused. The lace veil made it difficult for him to be sure, but his eyes were growing accustomed to the dim lighting. He could see her features somewhat: large eyes, a delicate chin, and lips curving upward.

"Why would I do such a thing?"

The train jerked, pulling away from the platform, slowly gathering speed. With her hands in her lap, she sat very still, looking him over, from his boots upward.

"Take off your coat, *Monsieur*. Be comfortable."

Rising, she first drew down the blind upon the outer window and then upon the smaller pane of glass within the door leading to the corridor. She clicked its lock closed.

Sitting beside him, he caught her scent—an arousing blend of orchids and orange blossom with a smoky, woody undertone. His heart lurched before beating faster.

As she placed her hand upon his thigh, the bulb flickered again and fizzed out.

CHAPTER TWO

Dartmoor, 1st December

It was hardly surprising that Reverend Wapshot's wife looked forward to her weekly invitation to Wulverton Hall. Lady Marguerite de Wolfe, widow of the late viscount's younger son, Lord Edward, was generous in her provision of afternoon tea, and Griselda Wapshot was exce fond of all varieties of cake.

Today's *tête-à-tête* was, no doubt, proving especially rewarding as Lady Marguerite had received not one but two pieces of correspondence, each bearing a foreign stamp.

"The new viscount makes his return at last," sniffed Marguerite. "It seems he did not hear of his father's passing until a few weeks ago, the telegram having awaited him for some time at his bank." Setting aside the letter, she snapped a butter biscuit on her plate and proceeded to crumble it to a state of dust. "He must be frugal in his spending, at any rate, since he draws upon his account so rarely."

Marguerite was aware that any opinion she wished to keep private should not be discussed in front of Griselda but, this morning, she could not contain her irritation.

"And does he travel alone?" Griselda shot her a bird-like look of inquiry.

"There's no wife that I know of." Marguerite added a lump of sugar to her cup and stirred vigorously before summoning a white-capped maid.

"More hot water, Betsy." She waved her hand at the diminishing platters. "And more of these. Strawberry jam rather than raspberry, if you please."

"If he's married, won't it put an end to your Hugo's expectations?" Griselda applied her spoon to the clotted cream; a scone was not worthy of the name unless sufficiently heaped.

Hugo's position as heir presumptive was widely known. He was next in line, should the new viscount fail to marry and bear a son to carry the title. The viscount's imminent return was a worry. Even if he'd avoided the married state all these years, bachelors of a certain age were likely to surprise one. He might take a notion to wed at last and sire a whole nursery.

They'd all be gossiping, no doubt, anticipating the dashing of Hugo's hopes. Her son was respected well enough but lacked strength of character. His father had been the same.

Even at a tender age, as Marguerite understood, the eldest son, Mallon, had commanded great respect among the moorlanders—and not just by dint of sporting the traditional dark hair and green eyes of the de Wolfe line. He'd ensured the rethatching of every tenant's dwelling, and the repair of several wells and stone walls on the estate.

However, coming down from Balliol College, he'd remained barely seven months under his father's roof before announcing his joining of Her Majesty's Field Forces, under Major General Roberts.

Marguerite felt a degree of sympathy. Her late father-in-law had been a cold fish. Even the birth of Hugo had done little to melt the *froideur* of his heart.

She smoothed her skirts. "But, of course, Hugo has a title and wealth in his own right, being the main beneficiary of my brother's will." She invited Mrs. Wapshot to another macaroon. "I wrote over a year ago to invite his widow to the hall. With no family of her own, it will be lonely for her at the château, beautiful as it is."

Mrs. Wapshot nodded, soaking up every detail, Marguerite knew, for careful repetition.

Naturally, Marguerite was selective in what she chose to share. There was no need, for example, for the reverend's wife to hear about her sister-in-law Geneviève's modest beginnings. Marguerite's brother, Maxim, had been over thirty years her senior and there was little doubt that Geneviève's physical charms had inspired the marriage. Her family connections were best overlooked and she'd brought not a penny to the match.

Having entered the house as companion to Marguerite's mother, the dowager countess, she would, at least, have learnt how to comport herself. If the girl proved suitable, Hugo might do well to marry her himself, thereby consolidating the income from the family estate.

Really, what had Maxim been thinking, bequeathing to his young wife such a significant portion of the vine-yard's revenue for the duration of her lifetime? She might claim the benefit of it for another fifty years!

Marguerite pictured herself leaving the damp and dreary moor and returning to the glorious sunshine of her native land, to long summers of picnics and plucking figs and lemons fresh from the tree.

One should hardly rejoice at such things, but the passing of her brother might be viewed as a blessing. His roguish behavior had brought disrepute on the family name. Under her guidance, Hugo would make amends. Moreover, her grandchildren would be born as generations before them, as true little French men and women, under the roof of Château Rosseline.

As soon as the festive period concluded and she'd overseen the viscount's acquaintance with his nephew, she would make plans.

There was a knock at the door, and a stooped figure shuffled in, giving a slight bow. "Excuse me, m'lady. There's a gentleman to see you. I've put him in the library, to await your convenience."

Marguerite sighed. "You know I don't see casual callers, Withers."

"'Tis Sergeant Hawky, m'lady." Placing the caller's card in her hand, his own shook a little.

Mrs. Wapshot swallowed her remaining piece of walnut cake. "Nothing...wrong?"

"Not at all, Griselda!" Marguerite rose from her seat to encourage her guest's departure.

Not for the first time, Marguerite lamented that life had brought her to such a remote and unsophisticated location. Genteel Society was sadly lacking, requiring her reconciliation to company she would otherwise have shunned.

CHAPTER THREE

GENEVIÈVE, Countess Rosseline, had slept for most of the journey, enfolded in her green velvet travelling cloak. She'd been travelling on the train from Dover since late the night before and the prior crossing from Calais had made her thoroughly sick, preventing even the slightest rest.

She'd considered taking a sojourn in London but had deemed it unnecessary after taking some days in Paris. What was there to see or do or purchase in London that could not be attained with infinite superiority in France's capital? Paris was an enchanting place, Geneviève finding herself delighted by its restaurants, ateliers, and galleries. She'd even ascended La Tour Eiffel, to look out over the great city. Regrettable that she'd had only her maid, Lisette, for company.

Many times, she'd asked Maxim to bring her to Paris, but there had always been some excuse. He'd preferred to leave her at the château on his expeditions, which he'd professed were purely for business. Geneviève had known better than to pry.

Of course, as beautiful as Paris was, it was not her home. If any place deserved that name, it was Château Rosseline.

Geneviève's earliest years had been a kaleidoscope of colorful commotion, of theatre dressing rooms and the vivid characters who inhabited them. Trailing the skirts of her mother, Antoinette Villiers, the darling of the Marseille stage, young Geneviève learnt not just to dance and sing and to speak the Italian and English tongues, but how to charm! There were flowers and chocolates and champagne, delivered by various hopeful men, and then there was just one—who sent jewels instead of trifles.

Geneviève was but eight years old when her mother took her to stay with the nuns of Santa Clotilde Magdalena. Gone were the gaudy delights and the soft, fragrant embraces of the lovely Antoinette. Geneviève shed nightly tears for her absent *maman*, until she realized that tears were wasted when there was no one to heed them. By the time she joined the household of the Comte Rosseline, at the age of fifteen, she'd long given up the act of weeping.

It was not the first time the château had embraced its civic duty in relieving the convent of one of its foundlings. With the nuns, Geneviève had learnt the advantage of appearing meek to avoid the cane across her palms—a performance she had refined during her years as companion to the Dowager Countess Rosseline. Geneviève's manners were impeccable and, unlike so many young ladies, she did not gabble.

After some years of fulfilling her responsibilities to the aging comtesse, including a fitting display of grief at her graveside, Geneviève had resigned herself to satisfying a new set of duties in the service of the count. Following his mother's death, there'd been no-one to curb his excesses. Only a worrisome chest infection had achieved that.

Maxim had seen her as a palatable diversion, with just the bedside manner he craved. Who else would read to him so exquisitely from the books he'd once hidden from his mother, and then act out the scenes within?

Had it been so wrong of her to tell the count he'd fathered an heir? A kindness, rather, for didn't all men seek to face the Reaper believing their legacy ensured? Having no father to protect her nor mother to arrange the delicate matter of a husband, she'd been obliged to make her way as best she could. If deceit were the result of necessity, then how could it be wicked?

Even if it were, Geneviève concluded, it could hardly be her fault, since all were slaves to baser instincts. From the fateful conjunction of the serpent and the apple, it had been so. In this case, to sin now and then was only natural.

Thus, had Geneviève become the comtesse and thought herself the luckiest of women. Château Rosseline had no match in grandeur. Its gardens were a lush paradise. Its vineyards bountiful. Even with Maxim's fondness for gambling, the coffers remained full.

As companion to the dowager, Geneviève had

accepted her lowly position. As wife to the count, she'd imagined taking *pastis* and *macarons* with the nobility of Marseille and Avignon. Yes, her background was humble, but she was Comtesse! It had been a bitter realization that she was still viewed as a barefaced upstart. The men, at least, had shown some courtesy, though she was too often obliged to smack their hands from where they strayed.

The women were another matter entirely. While Maxim was alive, she'd found them inclined to turn their backs. In widowhood, even after a suitable period of mourning had passed, Geneviève's soirées were politely declined, and those who'd tolerated her before, refused to receive her in their homes.

Becoming mistress of the château had been a dream. The reality had turned to ash in her mouth.

Geneviève had contemplated packing her bags and leaving it all behind, to begin a new life in glittering Paris. But why should she forfeit the place she loved best in all the world?

One way or another, I'll marry Maxim's heir, and return as the comtesse, twice-chosen! They think they've won, driving me from the home they believe I don't deserve—the place that has been my one true haven—but I won't cower before those condescending harpies. I shall return with my head held high, and they may choke on their tongues!

LISETTE WOKE HER AT EXETER, where they found the coachman waiting. Rain having clogged the road with mud, Geneviève was obliged to vault over a puddle to reach the step, swinging her valise into the carriage before her.

To start with, the horses kept a brisk pace, heading west past shorn fields between harvest and sowing. Now, they were ascending, laboring upward as the last portion of the afternoon faded.

The lowering sun lent the barren landscape a softness, giving the distant veins of water running upon its hillsides a Titian hue and bringing out the deeper russet tones of the bracken. There was little birdsong as the hedgerows and trees grew sparser, rowan and hawthorn giving way to gorse and twisted hazels.

Lisette was drowsing, her head lolling to her shoulder with the rocking motion of the coach. How fortunate it had been that Geneviève had already sent her away, that evening on the train. Geneviève continued to gaze out of the window but her thoughts were all of remembrance.

With a day's stubble upon his face and dark hair curling over his collar, the man who'd entered her carriage had looked more gypsy than gentleman, though his accent had belied that. He'd thought nothing of her hearing his curses at finding the compartment already taken. She'd known men like the stranger among her husband Maxim's acquaintance. There had been some baron or other with a voice of similar, brisk cadence.

Geneviève knew that a man liked to conquer a virgin's innocence, and had presented herself as such when Maxim had finally taken her to his bed. The handsome cellar-hand at the château could have told a different tale, of course, and the stranger upon the train might have doubted that she'd ever been so innocent.

He'd looked like a man who knew how to pleasure a woman. Since her widowhood, she'd taken a handful of lovers but each had left her wanting. And then he had appeared, as if sent to assuage her greedy, reckless soul.

She'd noticed his boots before anything else, long and black, in expensive leather. Then, the buckskin of his breeches and the longer length of his jacket. Nothing of the current fashion. Yet, he was boldly attractive, with a straight nose and high cheekbones.

Her choice had been one of impulse, and she'd been able to think of little else since. Sitting astride him, brushing his cock with the soft fur of her sex, teasing him as he kissed the length of her throat, then her ear. Pushing down the muslin of her camisole, he'd taken her breast wholly into his mouth, suckling so hard she'd felt it in her womb—that part of her clenching with a hunger over which she'd had no control. He'd pulled her onto his thickness, and she'd cried with the joy of it.

His tongue, his hands, had found each place of pleasure, drawing it from her until she was mindless with desire, pliant beneath his sweat-slicked body. He'd claimed his fill, then roused himself to take again.

At last, they'd slept, he on one side of the banquette and she on the other. When she'd woken, to the whistle of the train arriving at Paris's Gare de Lyon, he'd gone. In most ways, it had been a relief. The encounter had been spontaneous, and such liaisons were best suited to the mystery of the night.

Nevertheless, the memory of his lovemaking haunted her—or his fucking, she should say. Geneviève liked to call a thing by its proper name. She was not one for romanticism. It had also been an act of defiance, her coupling with a stranger—a delicious surrender. Submission to dark eyes and hands large and purposeful, and to that craving, hungry mouth which had left her lips bruised. Skin raked by the fine stubble of his jaw. Him tasting her, piece by piece.

The coach jolted, making its way higher, the landscape changing as they climbed. The moon was riding a clear sky, deepest black and dotted with dazzling pinpricks. Beneath, the moor was stark—an expanse of gray, its flatness punctuated by gentle hills and the outline of dark rocks.

They passed small clumps of buildings and then fewer, until there was barely a hut, and she wondered if the coachman could be taking them to the right place. Somewhere on the air was the rustle of falling leaves, though there seemed to be few trees to make such a sound possible.

And then the road twisted and dipped and the moonlight almost disappeared, for they were passing between a dense snarl of woodland—a strangled tangle of over-crowded branches, struggling against one another, deformed and disfigured. There was a smell of decay, old leaves heaped deep, and rotting stumps protruding like blackened teeth.

The wind, somewhere above, was riding melancholy over the dark mass, making it creak and rub, the trees scratching at one another.

Geneviève drew back from the window, wishing no longer to look, fearing suddenly what might be looking back, unseen.

It was a relief to emerge once more into the open, crossing a bridge before the track rose again.

Lisette jumped awake as they pitched through a series of particularly large potholes.

"Sommes-nous presque là, Comtesse?" Lisette smothered her yawn, asking if their destination were far off.

"Nous arriverons bientôt," Geneviève replied, hoping it might be true that they would soon arrive.

At last, they slowed to negotiate the turn through tall, iron gates, leading to a long avenue of yew trees. The branches had been pushed hard, mangled to become clutching fingers from one of the darker fairy tales, silhouetted beneath a sky turned threatening. The wind had risen, sending clouds across the moon.

Wulverton Hall brooded beneath a veil of ivy. There were four turrets in all, forbidding towers looming upward. Light spilt out across the gravel from the narrow windows on either side of the grand entrance. A coat of arms had long ago been engraved into the archway, though the stone was too considerably weathered for Geneviève to discern its emblem. A lion's head? No, a wolf, of course, Wulverton Hall being the seat of the Devonshire de Wolfes.

What shall we discover inside? Not love, for what good is that? A man of position and wealth? Now, that I can find use for. A husband so besotted that he'll bend to my every whim? Even better.

The coachman deposited their baggage and,

stamping her feet against the cold, Geneviève waited for the door to open.

THE BUTLER, who introduced himself as Withers, was tall and thin and stooped, and as sombre in appearance as the house itself. The family had evidently retired, leaving the aged retainer to wait up for her arrival.

Good, thought Geneviève, for she felt wrinkled and rumpled from travelling.

He closed the door with a doom-filled thud, turning the great key in the lock. All was silent, save for the creaking tick of a grandfather clock and the butler's labored wheeze.

"This'n way, Madam." The frail light of his lamp flickered upon the walls of the cavernous hall, from which long-dead de Wolfes looked down, dim and disapproving. However magnificent the plaster ceilings had once been, the damp had gotten to them. Wulverton Hall's glory was not just faded but peeling at the edges and flaking onto the carpets—an impression only consolidated as Geneviève followed the butler's shuffle up the stairs and along the upper passage, panelled in dark oak beneath time-blackened rafters.

A dusty tapestry, its threads coming loose along the lower edge, hung the length of the corridor—a maritime scene, as far as Geneviève could tell, though it was hard to say, reliant upon the limited illumination of Withers's lamp. A strange choice, since they were far from the sea here, on the high plateau of this remote moor.

There were definitely ships, majestic in full sail, and each bearing a name: Uriel, Raphael, Ramiel... Most of the embroidered lettering was too faded for her to read properly, but those were names of angels, weren't they?

And at the top of the hanging, more wording, sewn in silver thread, gold and green: de Winter, St. Hèver, de Russe, du Bois. Further names stretched on. Names of *la noblesse*. The Marquis de Winter's son had won ten thousand Francs from Maxim at the card table one night. And Geneviève had seen pictures of the Duchesse St. Hèver in the pages of *La Nouvelle Mode*. Her hats, so elegantly styled, were beyond compare.

What strangeness! For wasn't this the residence of an English family? To have some ancient connection in French lineage was common enough, but it seemed bizarre to display the names of other dynasties in one's home. There would be some story, of course, and she would be obliged to listen and exclaim prettily on how marvellous it was that the de Wolfe family was so well connected. Marguerite, Maxim's sister, would make the most of it, no doubt. Perhaps it had been she who had found this tattered piece of cloth and placed it along the wall.

As they reached the end of the passage, Withers stopped to turn the handle of a door.

"Yer room, Madam."

Fortunately, her bedchamber was far more charming. The curtains at each corner of the bed matched those at the window and the upholstery on the little

27

sofa by the hearth—ivory patterned with pink roses. She was relieved to see kindling had been set, with logs beside.

As the butler directed her to a tray of refreshments left upon the cabinet, Geneviève gave him her sweetest smile and a guinea from her purse. Decrepit he might be, but keeping on his good side was sure to prove useful. A comfortable stay relied upon the favor of such servants; the alternative was lukewarm water for washing and an age to wait if she ordered tea.

It was with relief that Geneviève at last divested herself of her travelling clothes. Though she'd had Lisette lace her corset loosely, it remained a garment she would happily have thrown upon the fire.

Yawning, she drew back the embroidered coverlet and climbed the steps to enter her bed. It complained noisily and sagged toward the middle but she'd slept in worse.

At the convent of Santa Clotilde Magdalena, Geneviève's bed had been a simple, slatted affair and her mattress stuffed with horsehair.

How far she'd come! And how far she intended still to rise. She would surely entice Maxim's heir to propose marriage before the Twelfth Night of the festive season. Charming men had never presented difficulty. She doubted this young man would be any different.

With that thought, she lay her head upon her pillow and indulged the fantasy which had grown stronger with each passing day.

With Hugo, the new Comte Rosseline at her side, those who had shunned her would surely change their tune. *The Baroness de Boulainville may once have encouraged the ladies of her circle to make me feel unwelcomed in the Society that is part of my home, but I shall show her that I'm not beaten. I shall take my place among them, and they shall beg for my invitations! I shall host the grandest of balls, and I shall welcome all but her!*

To the rising howl of the wind, Geneviève closed her eyes and dreamt of sour matrons curtsying as she passed.

CHAPTER FOUR

"Whortleberry ham and furze-blossom money," declared Lisette, placing the breakfast tray upon the bed. "Madame Fuddleby learn me!" Walking over to the curtains, she gave them a good yank, creating a whirl of dust that made them cough.

"Very good, Lisette—except that it's jam and honey!"

Teaching her some English had seemed a sensible idea, for who knew how long they'd be at Wulverton. It would be rather awful for Lisette if she had no mastery of the language at all.

Geneviève chose the warmest of her dressing gowns before climbing out of bed. Slathering her toast, she took a slice to the window. Great spatters of rain were obscuring the view, slapping steadily against the panes, which misted up as Geneviève attempted to peer through.

"Sleet coming," said Lisette. "Then snow, Madame Fuddleby says."

"I'm sure," mused Geneviève. If it was anywhere near

as cold outside as it was in her bedroom, she was surprised the whole moor wasn't iced over.

Finishing the light repast, she dressed in an emerald skirt of fine woven wool and a matching jacket, nipped at the waist, with pleats to the rear and black beading through the bodice. It had been among the items she'd most recently purchased in Paris, elegant and understated.

Geneviève assumed that her sister-in-law knew every detail of her background, but first impressions were important. Marguerite had been most solicitous in her invitation to Geneviève. In fact, of all Maxim's relatives, she'd been the only one to send a telegram of congratulation on their marriage. Now, it was time to face her and assess the kind of woman she dealt with. Would Lady Marguerite be a hindrance to Geneviève's plans or an ally?

As Geneviève sauntered from her room, negotiating once more the long and draughty corridor, she noted that the tapestry of ships looked no less shabby by daylight. Several sections were quite threadbare, although the name of de Wolfe had been repaired and made bolder, taking pride of place in the upper center of the border.

Wulverton Hall was neither a place of warmth nor of particular comfort. However, Marguerite's letters promised a gracious welcome.

Geneviève found the door of the morning room open and was met by an impression of vibrant colors and an amount of clutter, as if no one had ever thrown anything away. The de Wolfes had long been keen on dogs and horses, and combinations of the two, judging by the paintings and figurines littered abundantly. Even the family portraits seemed to figure one or the other, their faces often more charming than their owners.

"*Putain de feu diabolique*!" came a voice from beyond the sofa. A woman was on her knees, prodding the burning logs with a poker and uttering the most inventive curses. The reason was clear, smoke was billowing into the room.

"Essaie ceci," cried Geneviève, running forward with a newspaper. Falling to the floor, she wafted frantically, then had the idea of opening the window. The draught worked immediately, drawing the fumes up the chimney.

"*Cheminée démoniaque!*" The woman sat back on her heels, passing the back of her hand across her forehead. "This fireplace will be the death of me!"

"I do hope not," said Geneviève, helping her hostess to her feet. "I'm very much hoping to know you better."

"Ah! Geneviève!" cried Lady Marguerite, pulling her into a kiss for each cheek.

Geneviève saw the resemblance to Maxim at once. Her hostess had the same pale blue eyes, alight with intelligence. Her hair was fairer than Maxim's had been and her skin paler, but the slender Rosseline nose was there, and the same haughty bearing.

"*Mon Dieu*! The soot! Forgive me, what a beginning! And I'd hoped to have the *café au lait* ready for you when you came down." Lady Marguerite pulled the rope beside the fireplace. "Or would you prefer *un chocolat chaud*? I often take that myself at this time."

"Either would be delightful," said Geneviève, settling into a seat. "It's so wonderful to be here, finally meeting you. I must thank you, before anything else, for your thoughtful letters. My marriage to your brother must have come as a surprise…"

Geneviève had practiced her little speech many times but now faced with delivering it, she had the grace to blush. Her hostess was one of the few to have shown Geneviève consideration. The fabrication of small lies had become second nature to Geneviève, but it did seem a shame to begin her relationship with Marguerite under a veil of artifice. Nevertheless, until she knew more of her sister-in-law, it was safest to keep to her intended script.

"It was a surprise for me, as well. You know how I came to the château, of course, and I never expected…"

"Now, now," said Lady Marguerite, patting Geneviève's hand. "We are women of the world and do not need to explain ourselves. You made Maxim happy, I believe, and for that, I thank you."

A maid arrived at that moment, and her ladyship motioned for her to place the tray between them. "We are widows together and shall keep our husbands in our hearts as we embrace whatever life has next in store for us."

"Beautifully put," said Geneviève, accepting her cup. "You're all kindness."

"Only in part, and please call me Marguerite since we're now sisters. Our meeting is long overdue, and I assure you that I have my reasons for bringing you from the sunshine of our dear Château Rosseline to this drear place."

Geneviève replaced her cup upon its saucer. "I'm sure Maxim would have been pleased to see us become friends. I can think of nowhere else I'd rather be, especially as the festive season begins. I have no family of my own—at least none who care where I am or what happens to me."

Though it was only what she'd rehearsed, Geneviève's heart tightened, for there was truth in the sentimental little speech. However, she shook off her momentary self-pity. "It touches me greatly that you've welcomed me into your family."

"I fear there won't be much excitement. It's best to have modest expectations." Lady Marguerite sighed. "You and I probably have more brains and charm between us than the collective society of the entire moor."

"Then we shall make our own amusement," conceded Geneviève. "And I look forward to meeting your son, of course."

"Ah, yes! I have a feeling Hugo will be quite taken with you." Lady Marguerite gave a knowing smile. "And another will be joining us. With the late viscount's passing, we await the arrival of his elder son, from far abroad." She leaned forward in a confiding manner. "An estrangement, you know, as can happen between headstrong men."

Geneviève was about to inquire further when there was a flurry of wagging, shaggy tails, and lolling tongues and hot breath snuffling. Two great, gray wolfhounds had rushed eagerly toward the fire and were dipping their heads to the tray and the rug and into her lap, in search of crumbs.

"Tootle! Muffin! Stop that!"

Lord Hugo had entered the room, tall and slender and as blue-eyed and blond as a baby, with a smooth chin to match. It seemed that he'd taken all his mother's looks, for he bore no resemblance to any of the de Wolfe ancestors in the portraits she'd surveyed.

Geneviève rose to accept his welcome kiss, placed shyly upon her hand.

"What a pleasure to meet you…aunt, Countess… Aunt Geneviève." Hugo appeared flustered.

"Just Geneviève, please, and certainly not Aunt, since I'm barely five years older than yourself."

"Of course, Geneviève." Hugo took a seat beside her, and the dogs trotted over to lie at his feet. "I'm so glad you're here. I never knew my uncle, but I hope you'll tell me all about him." He gave each wolfhound a scratch behind the ears. "My mother mentions he had a reputation for being degenerate but she's far too proper to reveal the details."

Geneviève noticed that Marguerite's eyes slid away to gaze at something of imaginary interest beyond the window.

"Maxim lived life to the full." Geneviève assumed a forlorn expression, as she hoped was appropriate for a grieving widow. "My only regret is that we lacked sufficient time for me to give him the son he wished for." She extracted her handkerchief, pressing it to the corner of her eye. "However, meeting you, I see that we can rest easy. The estate will be in good hands."

Hugo's cheeks reddened. "I shall do my best." He gratefully accepted a cup from Withers, burying his face below the rim.

"My brother's solicitor forwarded the terms to us some months ago, soon after your letter arrived," said Lady Marguerite, betraying no reluctance to broach the subject. "Maxim was most generous in his provision for you."

"He was." Geneviève shook her head at an offered plate of tiny sandwiches. "Even if I marry again, I keep my share of the vineyard's income. My husband was so thoughtful."

And rightly so, Geneviève couldn't help thinking. Of course, she was grateful for his consideration of her future and her happiness, but the settlement was what she deserved, having paid for it with her body.

Marguerite seemed desirous of pursuing the topic, but Hugo interrupted her with a cough.

"And how do you find the moors?"

"Oh! So wild and beautiful!" Geneviève had learnt a particular way of making her eyes sparkle (thinking of the diamonds in her jewel case proved most efficacious) and employed it now. "Meanwhile, Wulverton Hall is so cozy and full of history. Quite astonishing!"

His lips tugged into a small smile. "How diplomatic you are, and I suppose you've noticed nothing of the draught coming in at your bedroom window and the unremitting gray landscape beyond it."

Geneviève laughed charmingly at Hugo's joke. "We

take for granted what we see every day. It can require the novelty of new experiences and new faces to awaken us to a passion for living." She gave him the full benefit of her lashes, sweeping them in an alluring flutter.

"Not much to get excited about here," replied Hugo. "Only good for mutton and wool, and I don't see myself as a sheep farmer."

"But it's an ancient place, your moor? And the de Wolfes of Wulverton Hall are well-respected. I should like to learn everything." Geneviève inched a little closer, ensuring that Hugo's knee was in danger of touching hers.

He coughed again and shifted, which inspired Muffin (or perhaps it was Tootle) to lay his great, furry head on his master's knee.

"I hear your coachman took the old turnpike road through Postbridge last night, past Wistman's Wood." Hugo popped a ham sandwich onto his plate. "A daring soul indeed, for few will cross the bridge after dark."

"The driver kept a brisk pace, but I thought it only his desire to reach his destination."

Hugo tore the sandwich into halves, each piece disappearing between salivating canine jaws. "You may be right. He was an Exeter man, after all. They don't know all our superstitions."

"Superstitions are just peasant fears, are they not? As a modern man, you don't believe in them, I'm sure." Geneviève assumed her most earnest expression.

"Well, I don't give credence to such tales in general." Hugo straightened his shoulders. "But Wistman's Wood is where old Dewer—the devil—is said to kennel his hounds. Huge shaggy dogs, they say, like wolves, with blood-red eyes, huge yellow fangs, and an insatiable hunger for human flesh and souls! His Wisht Hounds sniff out those walking the moor for the chance of chasing them to their deaths off the top of the great crag of Dewerstone."

"My goodness!" Geneviève wetted her lips, then parted them becomingly in an expression of astonishment.

"Really, Hugo!" Lady Marguerite interjected. "You're talking nonsense."

"You may be right, Mama, but I tried taking Muffin and Tootle for a walk near there and they were utterly obstinate. Wouldn't lay a paw over the threshold." He looked perturbed, reaching down to give each dog a comforting pat. "I don't much like taking the car that way either."

Then, like the sun appearing from behind the clouds, his face just as quickly brightened. "It's a nifty little mover. Ten horse-power, you know. A Wolseley two-cylinder. Goes like a beauty!"

Geneviève applied herself to appropriate admiration. "How daring you are! Taking the wheel of one of those thrilling machines!" She hoped she wasn't laying it on too thick. "I don't believe anything could frighten you, Hugo—whatever people say about that bridge or the woods or those awful hounds."

Hugo's color quickly rose again. "One can't be too careful. There have been vehicles forced off the road, and one feels something strange—as if hidden eyes were watching you. Most uncanny." He shifted in his seat.

"I was driving back from Moretonhampstead just the other week, running late, you know. Not wanting to miss the dinner gong, I took the most direct route, although it meant going through Postbridge. There was a frost coming on, so I had my thick gloves and heaviest coat. As I came close to the bridge, it got an awful lot chillier."

Geneviève nodded and touched her hand to his. Hugo seemed intent on telling his story but had grown rather pale.

"The Wolseley's lamps aren't at all bad—acetylene you know, and far better in the sort of dismal weather we get here—but you need to keep alert. I turned the bend and saw a pair of fiery eyes gleaming in the middle of the road. Damn near frightened the life out of me... pardon my language." He frowned, passing his hand through his hair.

"I grabbed the brake and, next thing I knew, I was sliding on the ice. Took all of my wits not to lose control completely."

"But it was just a deer, Hugo darling," Lady Marguerite broke in. "You told me so yourself. Bounded off through the grass in the direction of Archerton Bog."

"It was, but there was something else." Hugo appeared uncertain for a moment. "I hadn't wanted to say before, but just as the car began heading for the parapet of the bridge, I could have sworn I saw hands on the wheel. Someone else's hands, I mean." Hugo suddenly looked rather sick. "I kept trying to turn it back, but it was no use. I can still see them, those hands. Ghastly things!"

"How horrible!" Geneviève clutched Hugo's arm. "What a blessing you escaped unscathed!" She did her best to keep a straight face. Hugo was handsome enough, and pleasantly mannered, but so impression-able! A more perfect candidate for her husband-to-be could not have presented himself. "You're most brave! And to think I travelled that road myself unaware of its dangers!"

Hugo shook himself and smiled. "Ignore my nonsense. Too much imagination and the dark makes one jumpy, doesn't it?" He glanced out of the window. "The rain seems to be easing off, and I have a spare pair of goggles somewhere." The color had returned some-what to his face. "If I can tempt you, we might take out the Wolseley for a spin before luncheon."

"What a splendid idea," beamed Lady Marguerite. "But do wrap up warmly, my dears. We don't want you catching a chill, especially with all the festivities before us."

Geneviève wasted no time in rising.

Ha! Thank you, Lady Marguerite. Your assistance is noted, alongside your interest in my share of the vineyard. Hugo will do very well, and the Baroness de Boulainville and the rest of her coven can whistle for my favor when I return to my beloved château on his arm.

CHAPTER FIVE

HAVING FEARED a diet of tripe and boiled mutton, Geneviève was relieved to have found the fare at Wulverton Hall these past weeks quite palatable. Mrs. Fuddleby was adept in her baking, serving a particularly fine, spiced fruit tart, steaming hot from the oven, accompanied by Devonshire cream.

Having been mistress of her own household these recent years, there was some strain in being a guest once more, obliged to fit in with others' habits, though Geneviève boasted years of experience on that count.

She'd never slept well, nor enjoyed peaceful dreams. Too many memories crowding in, or an uneasy conscience, she supposed. So it had always been, and her nights at Wulverton Hall were no different.

Sometimes, it was Mother Superior who confounded her rest, commanding her to kneel upon the stone floor of the convent chapel and recite ten Hail Mary's for her sins. In others, she saw her mother, kissing her goodnight before sweeping from the room, never to return.

Geneviève rarely thought of Maxim, except to recall the expression on his face when she'd told him she was carrying his child. Of all the deceits Geneviève had employed, that troubled her the most. He'd been so very pleased, which had made it all the worse when she'd had to pretend the baby was lost. Was it divine punishment that those months of bedding had yielded no true pregnancy?

It was her habit to rise when rest eluded her, to fetch some small fancy or make a soothing drink. Lisette would have gone for her, of course, but it was the act of getting up that helped.

More than once, she'd encountered Withers on her twilight wanderings. Just the night before, she'd been stirring a pan of hot milk on Mrs. Fuddleby's stove when someone had passed outside the window with a lamp.

"Checking the premises are secure, Madam," he'd said, and made bold to scold her for being out of bed. "Ye'll catch cold."

"And you, Withers. Won't you catch it, too?" She'd been unable to hide her irritation.

"No, Madam, for I wuz born to the climate of the moor and its damp does me no harm. My family've lived on these'm lands for as many generations as the de Wolfes. B'aint none other with as much mist i' their blood."

He'd stood waiting for her to leave, and she'd heard him lock the door behind her. *Cheek!* she'd thought, supposing him a secret tippler of the cooking sherry. However, it wasn't her house and these were not her staff.

By day, Dr. and Mrs. Hissop were frequent visitors, and the Reverend Wapshot and his wife. Their amiable daughter, Beatrice, had played with Hugo from childhood and was undoubtedly in love with him. They were so evidently suited that Geneviève almost felt a pang of conscience at her wooing of the fair, cherub-faced Hugo. She doubted that a match between him and Beatrice would meet with Marguerite's approval but, were Hugo to assert himself, the courtship would surely blossom.

Sadly, Beatrice's heart was a necessary casualty of Geneviève's aspirations, to which she'd been applying herself assiduously.

Suggesting that they dress the Christmas tree together, she'd insisted on climbing daintily up the ladder, giving Hugo a glance of her slender ankles. Then, as fortune would have it, an unexpected lightness of head had obliged him to help her down and brought them tantalizingly eye-to-eye. Geneviève's lips had been ready to take advantage of their proximity to his, but Hugo had merely reddened and called for tea.

Thanks to their efforts, the balustrade of the grand staircase was festooned with ivy, and garlands hung in every room. There was no mantle unadorned with berry-bright holly. She'd anticipated the possibility of a kiss with each cluster of mistletoe hung, but Hugo remained an utter gentleman, no matter how Geneviève attempted to entice him.

He'd seen her in white lace and printed silks, in jaunty riding garb, and in sumptuous evening dresses. If he had a preference, it was unapparent.

"Such fragrance!" she'd declared, bending to inhale the scent of the lemons growing in the conservatory and offering him a fine view of her rounded derriere. "How I long to show you those that grow on the Rosseline estate." She'd faced him, moving scandalously close, touching her tongue to the seam of her lips while assuming an expression more innocent than the Virgin Mary—an attitude which had worked with sublime effectiveness during her days with Maxim. "Everything connected with that place of beauty is yours, as you know."

Hugo had remained oblivious.

He'd taken her on three drives about the nearby lanes, gathering greenery for their wreaths, each time without the least attempt at impropriety.

Today, Geneviève had decided that she'd initiate an overture. An accidental fall against his lap might do the trick, with her lips brushing his as she righted herself. Even Hugo—so naïve and bashful—could hardly fail to respond. The trip was to buy Christmas gifts, though Geneviève, naturally, had already purchased hers in Paris.

The weather was glorious, the craggy hillsides bathed in light beneath a crisp sky. As they made the return drive from Princetown, Hugo hinted at his purchase for Geneviève, and she began a coquettish game of guessing.

"Not lavender water or handkerchiefs, for those are

gifts for dedicated spinsters, and I shall never be one of those." She gave him the sort of smile that would have caused a man of greater experience to pull onto the verge without delay.

"Silk stockings?" Geneviève pressed a little closer as the Wolseley chugged slowly up the hill. "Or a night-gown of fine cambric edged with lace?" She ventured to touch his knee, as if to steady herself against the coming bend.

Good grief! Has it worked? Geneviève thought as Hugo directed the motor to the side of the road. Sadly, it was nothing of the sort.

"Call of nature," he mumbled, scurrying from the car and into the bushes.

Perhaps I should offer to go and hold it for him! fumed Geneviève. *Really, it's most tiresome and not at all flattering. A woman has her pride.*

They were on the crest of the hill and looking down upon Dartmoor's forbidding fortress. Despite the midday sun's warmth, she felt the chill of those gray prison walls, the silence of hopeless suffering, sorrow and hardship, and of tragic lives eaten by the years.

"First housed Napoleon's men, before our modern-day prisoners, you know," said Hugo, sliding onto his seat. "To get them out of the hulk ships. It looks impregnable but there are often escapes. This time of year, particularly."

"It makes me shudder to think of men doomed to spend their entire lives in such a place."

Geneviève had a fear of enclosed spaces. Long ago, Sister Maria Angelica had locked her in a cupboard for a misdemeanor Geneviève could not recall. She did remember the dark and the lack of air and her panting breaths, wondering if she'd be left there forever more.

"They've been beating the gorse for three convicts on the run, with only two back in custody." Hugo cast his eyes over the wide landscape before them. "The blighter might have made it to Plymouth and boarded a boat, but more likely, he's frozen from sleeping rough."

"And what will they do when they find him?" Geneviève, too, scanned the open moor below. The sun had melted the early morning frost, but as soon as the shadow of dusk fell, the temperature would drop severely.

"Shoot on sight, I wouldn't wonder." Hugo shrugged.

"Surely not, if he's unarmed!" Geneviève found herself indignant. He might be a murderer and deserve little mercy for his sins, but there were prisoners enough whose only crime was stealing to feed a hungry stomach, or a whole family of them.

Seeing her stricken face, his expression softened. He took her hand. "Not all have your generous heart, Countess."

Suddenly, the moment had come. He closed his eyes and leaned toward her, his lips soft as they met her own. The unexpected tenderness surprised her, and she forgot, almost, that a kiss required two. Hugo didn't seem to notice. The chasteness of the kiss and the color in his cheeks as he shifted in his seat, made her feel certain that it had been his first.

Thank goodness for that, she thought, having antici-pated the embrace for so long. However, relief at having finally gotten things moving along gave way to a slight ache about her heart—not for herself but for him. One's first kiss, she'd always believed, should be with someone for whom love is real, however temporary that state might be.

She intended to be a good wife to him, in all the ways she believed mattered to a man. If Hugo one day discovered the limitations of Geneviève's heart, she hoped her other charms would make up for his disappointment.

"I suppose we'd better be getting back," he said, as shy as he'd ever been.

Hugo engaged the first forward gear and they set off, gathering speed down the hill, which took them onward at a good clip across the flats. Had the wind been blowing, Geneviève might have lost her hat but the air was still and the sun all the warmer for it. It felt more like early autumn than December.

They entered a small thicket prior to the final approach, where the road forked before the track taking them to the gates of Wulverton. A coach and four was ahead, having just emerged from the avenue.

"Might be my old friend, Slagsby," said Hugo. "Mind you, he said he'd motor down. Fine fellow. A great one for japes—just like him to promise to show me his Prunel Phaeton and then turn up the old-fashioned way. Three-speed transmission, six horsepower and magneto ignition, and a nice shade of yellow. Jolly marvellous!"

Geneviève rolled her eyes. Here was the Hugo she'd

come to know. It was a rare conversation that didn't end in talk of motor cars.

"He's up at Oxford now. Clever chap. Grandpapa had hoped I'd go, but I've not the inclination for academic pursuits."

A variety of responses occurred to Geneviève but she bit her tongue.

"Could also be my uncle, though he's not due for a few days yet."

As they pulled up outside the main entrance, Hugo leapt out and came around to open Geneviève's door.

So very sweet, she thought. *We'll rub along all right. And he'll grow up—eventually. There are worse vices than an obsession with dogs and motor cars.* But she couldn't yet bring herself to enter the house. The weather was remarkably fine.

"I'll be in soon." She smiled. "I'll just walk over to the lake and back, to stretch my legs."

Waving her fingers, she set off before Hugo could suggest anything else, heading for the slight rise to the west of the hall. From there, the land dipped down in a hollow, where water formed a natural lake, encircled by rocks. It was a peaceful spot, hidden from the windows of the hall.

Approaching, she heard the splash of water, then saw a pile of clothes, boots and trousers, shirt and jacket, neatly folded.

Rather cold for a dip—but these local men are hardy fellows. Geneviève made to turn away but decided it wouldn't hurt to peep. It had been a while since she'd had the chance to admire a man in his naked glory, and she wondered if those hereabouts differed so much from their French counterparts.

If I crouch here, no one will see. In fact, it was much warmer in the hollow. The sun felt remarkably strong. She settled behind the rocks, peering round until she gained her view.

CHAPTER SIX

MALLON WADED INTO THE WATER, setting himself against the chill. A wader was calling, somewhere in the rushes —a curlew, perhaps. How often he'd closed his eyes in the desert and imagined the sun glinting on this very water, the russet of the hillsides and the low hum of insects on the lake. He'd always come here when he'd wanted to be alone. The hall might not have existed, hidden from view.

He thought back to the night on the train. He'd been wound tight, and a woman had been exactly what he'd needed. She'd been so very wet and so very willing. Just thinking of it made him ache. Not a single evening had passed without him recalling that encounter.

He'd taken her all the ways a man can have a woman; she'd certainly earned the money he'd left on the banquette.

Desperate to cool the fire in his loins from remembering that wicked passion, he encircled his girth. He squeezed as she had done, but it was impossible for him to replicate the sensation of her mouth.

Damn and damn!

There was only one thing for it. Swiftly, he ducked his shoulders under, then his head, rising with a gasp and more cursing. He swam further out, concentrating on propelling himself forward. He'd have her out of his system if it killed him. He'd never lost his head over a woman and he was damned if he'd allow it to happen now.

Not even a woman—but merely the remembrance of one! Bloody ridiculous!

Yet, he was thinking of her still, sitting across his lap, her velvet warmth inviting him in. She'd had a mole, beside her nipple, the contours of which he'd traced with his tongue as she'd moved her hips to take him deeper.

Reaching the shallows, he stood, finding his footing in the mud, the water lapping beneath his buttocks. He needed release.

Fisting himself, he stroked upward. Despite the water's coolness, he was burning hot, thinking of her as he pleasured himself.

With a final effort, Mallon groaned with satisfaction.

DARK HAIR, dripping wet, his body tanned.

She took in his hard angles and the curves of his muscles through his arms, back, and buttocks. A fine specimen of man, splendidly proportioned. Buttocks a woman would enjoy caressing. Arms strong enough to carry her and pin her beneath that masculine hardness.

He was standing, turned half away from her, the rhythm of his strokes unmistakable.

A labourer, she assumed, used to working in the sun, though what had possessed him to strip naked and take an icy dip she couldn't imagine.

With a jerk, he arched back and moaned. It made her smile. His body was delicious, and the lakeside secluded enough for a rendezvous.

Not that she would, or could...even she had her limits!

She looked up then, wanting to see his face, now that she'd had time to appreciate the rest of him.

The realization came to her like a punch in the stomach. She would know that jaw anywhere, although it was now clean shaven. His hair had also been groomed, no longer curling so wildly but long enough to tumble from his forehead. His nose was straight and his eyes a piercing green.

If there was any doubt in her mind, it was dispelled by the raised scar upon his right shoulder. Her own hands had touched such a wound, her mouth had kissed the puckered flesh. She'd unbuttoned his shirt and pushed it aside, pleading with him as he'd teased her.

A flush of heat rushed through her belly. That man. Her stranger. And he was here.

Lightheaded with fear, she crouched low, making her escape upon hands and knees.

CHAPTER SEVEN

How could it be! How was it that *he* was here? Rather, what cruel joke of fate that she was a guest in his house?

They were but six for dinner and to hide was impossible.

While Hugo attempted to engage her in conversation, Geneviève concentrated on cutting her trout into ever smaller morsels. However, she couldn't bring herself to swallow, nor to raise her face.

Encouraged by their kiss earlier that afternoon, Hugo was all attentiveness, venturing several times to brush his elbow with hers. Noting that she had little appetite, he suggested that Cook send up some broth if the fish was too off-putting. Geneviève did her best to smile and put his mind at ease, all the while aware it was the viscount, Lord Wulverton, she needed to convince of her composure.

I must pretend as I have so many times before. I am meek and obedient and without opinion. I will make him disbelieve his eyes. For how can I be the woman on the train? Such a thing is inconceivable.

The viscount seemed little inclined to speak but answered each question with a curt statement. Under Major General Roberts, he'd crossed the Shutargardan Pass into Afghanistan, to defeat the Afghan Army at Charasiab, and had fought in the Siege of Sherpur Cantonment during the uprising. He made nothing of his injury sustained at the Battle of Kandahar. His shoulder only pained him now and then, and had regained almost all mobility.

Of the years following his active service, he spoke even less. He'd settled in Constantinople, beside the sparkling Bosphorus, though how he'd spent his time there he declined to say.

At last, Marguerite invited them to withdraw. They'd take their brandy and coffee together in the adjoining room.

"Allow me," said Dr. Hissop, helping Geneviève rise from her chair. "How are you finding the moor, Countess? Not too quiet?"

"It's all I'd hoped for." She forced herself to smile—to respond as she must. "And you, doctor?" Wishing to keep her distance from the rest of the party, Geneviève guided him to stand near the window.

"My wife misses the liveliness of Exeter life while I find the moorland fascinating. I'm a lover of antiquities but lack the time or funds to travel to the ancient sites of Greece and Italy. Here, on our very doorstep, we have a wealth of history, cairns and barrows and stone circles. There are a great many on the moor—especially kistvaens, the stone-clad hollows where the ancients placed their dead. If you ever find yourself caught in a downpour, they make excellent hiding places to duck out of the rain."

"How intriguing." Geneviève's gaze travelled across the room. Marguerite had drawn the newcomer into conversation. Geneviève might endure another ten minutes before making an excuse to retire.

Dr. Hissop seemed to be warming to his subject. "The dwellers of the moor have many tales and customs also worthy of attention. Their folk superstitions are not always original, of course, except in the way they relate to local landmarks. The corpse-lights, for instance, which are said to lure the unwary into the mire."

"Ah, yes." Geneviève took a sip from her coffee cup. "We have the same in France, little dancing lights on the marshes which lead you to step where you should not and lose your way."

"Quite so," replied Dr. Hissop. "People think they're above such superstitions in our rational, modern century, with its motorized vehicles and moving cine-matographs, but if you find yourself alone on the moor after dark, you may find your mind wandering down paths illuminated more by fear than reason."

Geneviève turned her back a little more on the others across the room and urged the doctor to continue.

"Then, there's the Lych Way." Dr. Hissop's eyes were alight. "The medieval funeral path used to carry corpses across Dartmoor to their internment. Several of my patients swear they've seen ghostly processions, and without having taken a drop of liquor!"

Geneviève forced herself to laugh while stealing a furtive glance toward Lord Wulverton. Hugo was chattering away, but the viscount did not seem to be listening. Instead, he was looking over his balloon of Cognac —positively staring, in fact, and at Geneviève alone.

IT WAS SO strange to be back. Very little had changed. The same portraits hung upon the walls, and the same brocade curtains adorned the tall, mullioned windows. Even the furniture seemed to be in the same place it had been on the day he'd left.

Only his bedroom seemed different. Smaller than he remembered. The bed—having accommodated generations of de Wolfes—still sagged in the middle. Lying upon it now, he couldn't help but think of the last night he'd spent under its canopy. How eager he'd been to leave. Twenty-three years, and here he was again.

His father appeared to have kept the hall in good enough repair, which was some relief. Mallon had wondered what he might find on his return, a leaking roof, perhaps, or boarded windows.

Many of the staff were new, of course, but Withers was still here, and Mrs. Fuddleby. Mallon had poked his head into the kitchen briefly and been rewarded with a warm embrace from their cook. She'd grown slightly rounder about the middle but her manner toward him was just the same. To her, he suspected, he'd always be Master Mallon.

Marguerite had greeted him cordially, though hadn't quite been able to conceal her wariness at his arrival. It was only to be expected. She'd lived here more years than he had himself. It was her home as much as his, regardless of his title of ownership. He'd done his best to assure her that he intended no change in that regard. As Edward's widow, she would always have a home at Wulverton Hall.

What had most surprised him was the attractive widow in their midst. Marguerite had told him something of her sister-in-law, now re-entering Society— and with gusto, it seemed, since she'd put aside her black in favor of a red silk gown swept low across her shoulders.

She was most definitely his type, generous in the bosom and hips, and with a waist that beckoned a man's hands. Her lips, sensuously full and deeply rouged, begged not just to be kissed but held the promise of other acts.

Had they met in London, he'd have certainly attempted to bed her. He indulged a fleeting image of the countess without her dress—without any clothes at all. He wondered if she'd be amenable to placing those fleshy handfuls at his disposal. It would certainly bring an element of spice to the weeks ahead. Much as he loved the moor, his expectations were low regarding the company to be had. He feared a parade of idiots foisted upon him. A little diversion would be most welcome.

Marguerite had told him the countess was well-provided for, though Hugo had inherited the main assets of her late husband's estate. She wouldn't be seeking an extended stay, surely. Paris seemed more her style—a place for a young widow of means to find suitable entertainment.

However, as pleasurable as such a fling would be, he set the thought aside. He'd only just gotten back and there was a great deal for him to assess on the estate. Tempting as it was, he could do without the inconvenience of an entanglement.

God forbid she should misconstrue his intentions and attempt to secure a longer-term commitment. It was the furthest thing from Mallon's thoughts. Women such as her, with such pronounced sensuality, put him most in mind of his own mother, whose excess of carnality had led to her ruin.

Nevertheless, he was drawn to observe her, and to admire. Since retiring to the drawing room, she'd been speaking with the doctor—or listening rather, for the man had a liking for his own voice.

The gems at her ears caught the candlelight—delicate drops of crimson against the white of her throat. Her dark hair was lustrous, upswept and decorated with a lavishly plumed aigrette. Her eyes, meanwhile, were an unusual shade. He'd thought them grey at first, but closer inspection showed them to be silver-threaded violet, like sunlight on stormy seas.

Mallon could not place the connection, but she was familiar to him. Her English was proficient, though her accent was pronounced. She had surely never visited Constantinople but where else would he have met her?

In Paris, or during his time in London? A group of French had sat at the table adjacent to his at the Criterion. It had been too gaudy for his taste, but he'd heard it was a favorite with Conan Doyle. He'd read a copy of his book, *The Hound of the Baskervilles*. The man had apparently spent some time on the moor and heard its tales. The rendering had been eloquent, making Mallon all the more eager to see Wulverton once more.

She glanced over to him, then swiftly away, with the look of a deer caught in the headlamps of a carriage and not knowing which way to run. He'd been staring too intensely and had discomforted her, it seemed, though her manner of dressing indicated that she was a woman who liked to be admired.

He was tired and would have excused himself to his bed, but it seemed he must approach and make right his ill manners.

GENEVIÈVE HAD TURNED her back utterly, but it was too late. He was beside her. She'd been thinking only of the necessity of concealment. Now, hearing his voice, so deep and rich, heat assailed her body. He wore the starched formality of evening dress, but she was aware of the muscle and blood beneath. She remembered the weight of him above her and the taste of his sweat. Grasping the window ledge, she willed herself into composure.

Viscount Wulverton introduced himself with a bow and made the usual courtesies of asking after her health, her journey and as to whether her comforts were being met. How she answered, she couldn't have said but he seemed to accept all her replies.

His attention then turned to the doctor's research of the moor, and Hissop lowered his eyes in a show of modesty. "An interest I shared with the late viscount. I offer my deepest sympathies."

Mallon seemed to hesitate, as if finding difficulty in framing his words. "You attended him, I believe—at the end."

"I did little more than make him comfortable in the final hours," said the doctor.

Mallon grimaced. "He spoke of me, before passing?"

Dr. Hissop shook his head. "The stroke robbed him of speech." The doctor made bold to touch Mallon's arm. "No doubt, you were in his thoughts, though he was unable to express them."

Mallon stepped back a little, removing himself from the doctor's gesture of comfort. "No doubt…"

It was an awkward moment. Despite the brevity of her sojourn at the hall, even Geneviève was aware of the late viscount's estrangement from his son. Surely the doctor knew how things had stood between them. She was able to imagine some degree of Mallon's grief, likely tinged with regret, for years lost and sentiments unspoken.

Marguerite called for them to sit, and it was with relief that Geneviève took the seat offered on Hugo's far side. Resigning herself to Tootle placing his great paws across her feet was a fair exchange for being able to turn her face—at least partially—toward the hearth. Mallon lowered himself into an armchair, stretching his legs before him as he accepted more Cognac.

"I do hope Samuel hasn't been boring you, talking of his hobby." Mrs. Hissop gave a fluttery laugh. "Few share my husband's enthusiasm for the contemplation of ancient granite."

"My dear, I do not just admire the moor's beauty, I wish to protect it against our exploitation of its metal, stones, and minerals." The doctor protested with an exasperated expression.

Geneviève allowed Withers to replenish her cup and continued her contemplation of the flames.

"There's never been mining on Wulverton land," Mallon asserted.

Dr. Hissop was not to be deflected. "Nevertheless, the moor needs protection from man's greed. Were there no laws to govern its use, who knows what state it would come to."

"You might join the Preservation Association," chimed in Hugo. "The doctor always wants me to get involved but you'll do much better than me."

Mallon's voice seemed all the more resonant for following the light tones of his nephew. "I'm sure you're too modest Hugo but, of course, I'll support any noble-minded venture. We're only guardians, after all."

"My household visits to my patients have been a double blessing," Dr. Hissop continued, "For I've had not only the opportunity to heal their ills but to compile a catalog of their superstitions and tales."

"And very gruesome they are!" Mrs. Hissop gave a theatrical shudder. "Once dusk has come, I won't step more than a few feet from our door, knowing what I do!"

"I love a good ghost story!" said Hugo. "Very traditional at this time of year. Dr. Hissop, you'll oblige us?"

"If you wish it, of course." Taking a sip from his brandy, the doctor adjusted the cushion in his chair. He appeared to ponder a moment, before an earnest look settled upon him and, casting his eye to ensure that all gave attendance, he began.

"Some women bring grief upon those closest to them, while others are the victims of others' greed. Of Lady Mary Fitz, some say she was a murderess. Others, only that she was ill-used by those who might have given her protection."

He rested his chin upon his fingers. There was no doubt he had every ear, for the only other sound in the room was the crackling of the fire.

And yet, as Geneviève listened, she was aware of Lord Wulverton's continuing gaze upon her. Did he know or suspect where they had met before? Despite her caution, had she given herself away?

CHAPTER EIGHT

IT WAS a story Mallon had heard often enough when he was a lad. Back then, it had given him nightmares and had been effective in keeping him to his bed. To glance out of the window brought the risk of seeing Lady Mary's ghostly carriage, cursed with ever travelling the moor.

The countess looked pale, her brow furrowed in concentration, or anxiety—he couldn't decide. A handsome woman, though her shyness seemed at variance with her mode of attire.

"Those born from violent blood are often destined to tragedy," continued Dr. Hissop. "Poor Mary was cursed, perhaps even in her cradle, for her father was the most hated and feared of men. His degeneracy led him into insanity and the murder of two men, including his own closest friend, on the very doorstep of Fitzford House. In a final act of wickedness, he took his own life, ceasing the beat of his blackened heart with the last plunge of his dagger."

"Oh, Samuel!" gasped the doctor's wife. She gave a nervous laugh. "You'll be scaring us all from our wits!"

And those being in short supply, it would be foolhardy to mislay them, thought Mallon.

Agreeing to temper his language, the doctor continued, "At the age of nine, Mary found herself an orphan, under the care of the Earl of Northumberland, though what care there was is questionable, since his only concern seemed to be to lay hands on her fortune. She was no more than twelve when he married her to his brother, Sir Percy. At that tender age, none suspected her when he, the first of her doomed husbands, caught a fever out hunting."

The countess seemed to catch her breath at that. *Thinking of her husband*, Mallon supposed. He found himself looking at a stray wisp of hair at the nape of her neck.

"Just two months after wedding her second spouse, Thomas Darcy, she was again a widow and one might have thought a third husband would be wary but, at seventeen, Lady Mary was married once more. Sadly, the match was far from happy, Sir John Howard caring more for her fortune than aught else."

Dr. Hissop leaned forward in his chair. "By twenty-seven, she was widowed a third time, and there were rumors aplenty that she'd struck a deal with Beelzebub to rid herself of those husbands. Yet, she took a fourth down the aisle, though Sir Richard Grenville did so without realizing Mary had tied up her fortune. He gave her a son, but the marriage was as miserable as the last, and the two parted ways. Choosing never to marry again, Mary retired to Fitz House, accompanied by her son. However, more ill-luck was to come, as the Lord saw fit to take her beloved George.

"Overwhelmed by grief, Mary departed this world but, even then, was afforded no peace. Death and unhappiness had always followed her. The true extent of her sins we cannot know, but it's said that, at the stroke of midnight, she rides out across the moor in a coach made of her husbands' clattering bones."

One of the logs sparked, throwing out an ember to the old rug, but none moved to stamp it out, leaving it to smolder to a dark spot.

"To look upon her as she passes is to feel the Dark One's claw upon your neck. To accept a ride in her macabre carriage is to offer your soul to the same dark forces that hold hers in nightly torment. At her side bounds a coal-black hound, straight from the gates of hell, its eyes glowing with demonic fire, guiding her journey to Okehampton Castle. There, the dog plucks a single blade of grass and carries it in its mouth for their return to Fitz House. Night after night, she repeats her impossible mission, destined to ride the moor until every blade is plucked."

As the doctor uttered the last words, Mallon felt a shiver pass over him. It had been many years since he'd heard the legend but its telling still affected him, though the moor was full of such legends—of demon dogs especially. Of course, women were fickle creatures and Lady Mary surely no better than the rest, but what a life she'd led, deserving pity more than condemnation.

Not like his mother, whose particular brand of

inconstancy he'd found himself unable to forgive. Faithlessness not just to her husband but to her children, too. What sort of woman was capable of that?

After a few moments, Marguerite cleared her throat. She was looking decidedly uncomfortable. Of course, both the countess and Lady Marguerite were widows, and barely two years out of mourning. Marguerite had found the story inappropriate, no doubt—a fact which Dr. Hissop seemed suddenly to realize. He grew quite flustered, his hands fluttering as he gave an apology.

"Not at all." Marguerite smiled tightly. "But, permit us to lighten our mood—perhaps with a hand at bridge."

The matter was soon settled. Hugo, the doctor, and his wife completing the four, so that Mallon found himself alone with the French woman.

The story of Lady Mary seemed to have left her in a state of nerves, for she fumbled with her cup although he could see that she'd already drained it dry.

He was not one for excessive small-talk, but it was unavoidable until he might make his excuses—a long journey and his bed calling to him. However, she spoke before he had the chance to initiate any topic, rising to pronounce her desire to retire.

Mallon drew in his legs as she stepped past, but her skirts brushed his foot, and her perfume lifted to him — a heavy, musky, floral scent, woody, with a touch of citrus. Again, he was struck by the certainty of their having met before, something in the incline of her head or in the way she raised her chin.

"Goodnight, my Lord."

Even the cadence of her voice was familiar, melodious and sensual.

Get a grip on yourself, man! She's just a woman, born with a certain repertoire of charms and all the limitations of her sex.

He berated himself, yet he continued to think of her long after he, too, had climbed the stairs, to the cold expanse of his bed.

WITH HER DOOR closed behind her, Geneviève endeavoured to steady herself. She could have done with a large brandy rather than coffee, but the temptation would have been to knock it back in one gulp. Keeping a clear head had seemed the better option.

The fire was burning, taking some of the chill from the room, but Geneviève felt colder than she had even on her first night at Wulverton.

After helping her undress, Lisette left her mistress with an extra quilt and two warming pans between the sheets. Still, Geneviève could not melt the ice creeping through her veins.

The viscount had shown no indication of recognizing her. She'd know, she felt sure, by his manner if nothing else. He'd certainly looked her over most thoroughly, and he'd said nothing. Done nothing.

She was safe, wasn't she? At least for the time being. What next? Leave the house and abandon all her plans? She'd be damned if she would! All the work she'd put into Hugo, and only today making proper headway.

It had seemed the evening would never end, and that story! She detested the idea of women succumbing to hysterics, but it had taken all her willpower to remain in her seat. Only her ridiculous imagination, of course, but it had felt as if her soul were under scrutiny as Lady Mary's successive widowhoods were detailed.

Not that she'd murdered Maxim, though she'd helped his ease toward the end, administering the laudanum. She suppressed a shudder. Not even the angels would hold that against her, surely. She'd given only the dosage advised by Dr. Chevereau and not a drop more. A husband had been more useful to her living and breathing than beneath a headstone. She might be a countess in name, but her humble back-ground had prevented her from entering the *haute société* she craved. Even while Maxim had been alive, invitations had been scarce. As his widow, she'd ceased to exist in the eyes of Marseille's finest families.

She rubbed her feet together and pulled the quilts higher. From somewhere far away, she heard the grand-father clock chime midnight. Everyone would be in bed by now. She, too, needed her sleep. She was still young in years, but even Paris cosmetics could only do so much if a proper night's rest was lacking.

Her thoughts turned again to the problem of Lord Wulverton. No doubt, he enjoyed the company of a passionate bed partner as much as any man, but men were such hypocrites in these matters. What they welcomed from a tavern wench they tended to revile in women of their own class.

If he accused her of anything, she'd brazen it out.

Preposterous to suggest that a lady would act in such a manner. Inconceivable to charge the Comtesse Rosseline with such behavior! *Yes.* She would refute any such assertion. Wiser to present the face of a woman who had nothing to hide and nothing of which to be ashamed. Meekness was all very well, but perhaps a degree of charm would better serve.

She wiggled her toes inside the bed socks. Not that she felt shamed by her choices upon the train. She wouldn't say 'no', even now, were there the chance to have her cake and eat it too. A hot body in the bed would be more than welcome, and she'd already enjoyed proof of the gentleman's ability to satisfy. His blood clearly ran more than heated, judging by the little scene at the lake, and his physique was magnificent.

When she at last drifted to sleep, her dreams provided her with a lover whose hands were wonderfully warm, and far too skilled to be those of a man not yet twenty years upon the earth.

CHAPTER NINE

MALLON FOUND the countess in the library, curled into a highbacked chair beside a fire stoked and crackling, Hugo's wolfhounds lying beside. Through the window, Mallon could see his nephew bent over the engine of his contraption. He didn't understand this love of motor cars, but there were worse vices for a man.

She'd taken off her slippers to tuck her feet beneath her skirts and, warmed by the fire, had removed the shawl from her shoulders. Her fine wool dress was a modest silver-gray, embroidered at the waist and through the bodice. Tailored with her figure in mind, there was no hiding the swell of her bust and her hips. She was obscenely alluring, exuding a primal sexuality and a seasoned look. The sort of woman to have enjoyed her marital duties.

He stepped forward, bending to stroke each wolfhound behind the ears. "Like the dogs, you've found the most comfortable room in the house."

She mustn't have heard him approach, for she visibly started at the sound of his voice.

He took the seat opposite. "You're well rested, I hope?"

"I am, thank you." She smiled briefly, then turned back to her book without attempt to converse further.

She was under no obligation to humor him but, damn her, she *was* in his library. His grandfather's library, to be precise, since it had been that gentleman who'd purchased most of the editions—but his now. The entire place was his.

"You enjoy novels?" He nodded at the volume—a pristine copy of *Vanity Fair* he knew to be from the shelf of first editions.

"When they're written truthfully." She levelled her gaze to meet his, composing a serene expression.

"So, you admire its heroine for her honesty—Miss Sharp, isn't it? A rather scheming young woman, I recall." The book had been a favorite of his own in younger years, but he found himself wishing to provoke, if only for the pleasure of seeing how she would respond.

She betrayed a flash of pique, but her poise returned quickly enough. Easing her feet back into her dainty shoes, she sat up. There it was again, that slight inclination of her head, and her chin raised. Even when wrong-footed, she proclaimed restrained defiance.

"Quick wits and determination are praised in men. Rather unfair, don't you think, to deride them in women?" She leaned forward almost conspiratorially. "We're not all ninnies, Lord Wulverton."

He usually scorned such bluestocking talk, but the countess's physical charms more than made up for her confrontational manner. He much preferred this version of her to that of the previous evening, when she'd seemed afraid to engage him in any conversation. Now, she appeared all boldness.

"I wouldn't dare suggest such a thing." He gave her a placatory smile. "I'm sure you're as capable of judicial thinking as anyone you're likely to meet here. The moor is known more for its superstitions than its enlightenment."

He slid his booted feet closer to the hearth. "As you'll have gathered from Dr. Hissop's storytelling, this is a place of ghosts and otherworldly creatures, lore dating back to lost ages before man could write. In this place where a moonless night brings utter darkness, people must try to make sense of their fears. The mist is such that it's easy to imagine wraiths in the shifting light. One's vision is apt to twist and deceive, until a man's judgement is untrustworthy. Hardly surprising there are so many tales of demonic creatures."

He bent to pass her the volume he'd brought with him to the library to place it upon the shelf. She tilted it in her hands to read: *The Hound of the Baskervilles.*

"We're abundant in legends surrounding hounds, so it's likely that they inspired Arthur Conan Doyle in writing his book. There are nights when folk say they hear terrible howling on the moor. No one is rational in the face of that. It poisons all a man's courage."

He could see he'd caught her attention, drawing her forward.

"And what of you, Lord Wulverton? Are you a man of virtue and bravery, or do you cower under the shame of a wayward past? Will Old Dewer be sending his hounds to howl under your window?"

She widened her eyes in mock horror. Little could she know how near to the mark she'd struck.

So many years ago, he'd left the moor he loved. The recipients of his anger were buried cold in the soil, but his resentment remained. He'd squandered vitality and purpose, taking the easy escape into opium and hashish. Only his father's death had galvanized him to put aside his self-pity, to wean himself from those addictions which had blunted the edge of his torment but never released him from its grip.

As to whether he'd finally find peace, here, at Wulverton Hall, it remained to be seen. Some ghosts could never be laid to rest. If he had returned only to be lured into a new hell of remembrance, he was a damned man indeed.

GENEVIÈVE HAD NOTED Lord Wulverton's study of her as he'd sat in the armchair opposite, lounging back to cross one knee casually over the other. Evidently, the illumination on the train had been sufficiently lacking, preventing him from identifying her. To her great relief, he'd beheld her without demonstrating an inkling of recognition—by evening and, now, daylight.

He'd even been flirting with her, in the usual conde-scending way of a man assured of his superiority—

willing to indulge the whims of the female recipient. Until her pulling of his leg had seemed to tug at some corner of his conscience. A shadow had passed over him. Without doubt, he had his secrets—and he was welcome to them. She'd no interest in prying.

He jumped up abruptly, then busied himself with the fire, adding three more logs. "I'm hoping the devil may have some years yet to wait for my company."

Whatever gloom had overtaken him, he seemed not to wish her to see it.

"Perhaps you'd take me over the house," she said, laying aside the books and rising to stand beside him. "I've only seen the public rooms—nothing of those that have been shut up."

How tall he was and how large his hand, still gripping the poker. She thought of him gripping something else the day before, when he'd been unaware of her watching him.

She'd enjoyed observing him naked, but he was just as pleasing fully clothed, broad shoulders snug beneath his jacket, a waistcoat in paler gray, subtly worked with jacquard, and legs impossible in length. The tightness of his trousers concealed nothing of his muscular thighs, nor of what lay between them.

He led the way through hallways and galleries, through rooms decorated with heavy tapestries and ornate rugs— others bare but for dustsheets covering unused furniture.

"Watch your step," he warned, as the floor of the corridor dropped away. "It's the same with all these old houses. Various parts have been added over successive generations. For some reason, they didn't do the best job of making things line up."

Geneviève went to the end of the passage, where a long window displayed the northern vista. He came to join her, and they stood looking out at the expanse of bracken and the vast sky above, streaks of violet-gray moving fast against the paler blue of morning.

"I first thought it a rather desolate place—wild and empty," Geneviève admitted. "But it has its own beauty. At Rosseline, I love to explore. The vines occupy most of the land beneath the château, but there are hills and woodlands beyond which tempt me for whole days at a time. I often take a lunch in my saddlebag and go out riding."

"Our moor isn't like other places—not like other moors, even." He spoke softly. "You may walk easily for some hours without seeing another person or a dwelling, but the moor is not so barren as it seems. There is life here, in the streams and damp places, and on the hills, where the wild ponies roam. No man lacks for rabbit in his stew. People have lived here since Neolithic times. Not only their cairns and standing stones remain but their stories. We're closer to the past here. If you visit the circles at Hingston Hill or Yellowmead, you'll feel that. Like those stones of weathered granite, our moor-dwellers are resilient, born of the rock beneath their feet."

Geneviève turned to look up at him, wishing to see his expression. "And you've returned from your adventures to take on the mantle of your inheritance. Can you live without the conveniences of our modern century, without proper Society even?"

She made bold to taunt him. "Or perhaps you intend to bring electricity to Wulverton Hall and embrace the innovations of our age. Will you lure the London elite to your moorland retreat and make Wulverton the most sought-after invitation of the season?"

His smile was wry. "If you knew me better it would be the last thing you'd suggest. As to deprivation of comforts, you'd be surprised what I've lived without. In returning, I'm hoping to find…what I thought was lost to me."

"Ah, yes!" Geneviève sighed. "You seek the English idyll of nature—unspoilt, and so little inhabited. A place to feed the soul and heal its wounds. A place in which you acknowledge your belonging. It is what all your poets write of, is it not?"

He paused for some moments. "You might put it like that…"

A reverie appeared to envelop him and they stood in silence, until Geneviève wondered if he'd forgotten she was there at all.

How strangely he behaved.

At last, feeling restless, she coughed and shuffled her feet. It was sufficient to bring him back from wherever his mind had wandered to.

Smiling sweetly, Geneviève asked, "Your family have lived here many generations?"

There was a certain pride in his response. "Almost seven centuries—through fortunes good and bad. We can claim a certain fortitude. It's the de Wolfe motto in fact, *fortis in arduis*."

"Strength in times of trouble." Geneviève nodded in approval. "It's good to fight for what you desire."

She'd had time enough to learn that for herself. No matter what insults or ill judgements were cast upon her, she would endure. Above all things, she knew the importance of tenacity. Her heart was set on returning to Château Rosseline, and with Hugo, Maxim's heir, as her husband. That was something she intended to fight for. Viscount Wulverton had made no link between her and the woman on the Marseille train. All well and good. Let it remain that way. Meanwhile, she would act her part.

"And has your family braved much trouble?" Geneviève felt doubtful. What strife and suffering had this family endured?

Wulverton Hall was a modest residence in comparison to her château—with its priceless works of art and gilded ceilings, its great vineyards and extensive estates—but these de Wolfes appeared comfortable enough. The land made for poor farming, she imagined, but the sheep flourished. Wulverton Hall came with fifty thousand acres, Hugo had told her.

Moreover, life on the moor was so isolated from the machinations of politics. Any man with ambition would not live here, surely? It seemed more a place in which to hide from trouble. What strength could be needed when a person buried themselves in obscurity?

If Lord Wulverton had sensed her scepticism, he chose to ignore it.

"You'd be surprised, though it's true that my branch of the family cannot compare in fame to the great de Wolfes of Northumberland, nor to those who settled in Wolverhampton. My grandsire of many generations back, being the younger son of a younger son, chose to forge a new path here in Devonshire, sometime in the fourteenth century. His sheep farming was on a modest scale, though he established a dynasty that became stronger with passing decades. The Black Country de Wolfes have always been influential and wealthy, thanks, most recently, to the mining of coal."

"They are miners?" Geneviève could scarcely contain her mirth. Such a noble family, and involved with such a dirty occupation!

"Rather more than that." Again, he ignored her taunting manner. "One of my distant ancestors, Gaetan, having fought bravely at Hastings, was made First Earl of Wolverhampton by the Duke of Normandy himself— the first Norman King of England."

"Ah! So, you are proudly French! And the blood of brave warriors flows in your veins." The ships in the tapestry, and the names of prominent houses of French nobility now made a little more sense.

"I suppose a great many of us could make that claim, if we looked back far enough, but I don't think of myself as one of your countrymen—regardless of their many… notable qualities."

Geneviève gave him a sidelong glance. The English humor! She could not be quite certain, but it appeared he was now mocking her.

"You were telling me of your family's struggle, I

believe, Lord Wulverton. Please do continue. I love a tale of quest and tragedy. Do not be modest. If your people have lived up to their motto, then you should not be humble in telling of their... pluck, as you say. What sacrifices have they made in the name of love and honor?"

He paused again, for far longer than was needed to gather his thoughts.

Had she overstepped the mark? Really, he was the most difficult person—talkative one moment and then so melancholy, staring into nothingness.

At last, he looked down at her once more, his face very still. When he spoke, it was with a nonchalance that belied the intensity in his eyes.

"Our family suffered badly through the Civil War, being stripped of its finery by Cromwell's parliament. De Wolfes have always promised service to the crown, and we remained true to Charles I, fighting alongside Sir Bevil Grenvile and the other Royalists at the Battle of Sourton Down. Wulverton Hall was left half in ruins by the time the roundheads had finished tearing it apart. Those were hard years, I believe. Full of uncertainty."

"For that, I'm sorry." Geneviève felt a flush of shame at her hasty words. "To see one's home destroyed is tragedy indeed."

"Well, it turned out well enough in the end. With the Restoration, Charles II rewarded Allenby de Wolfe's loyalty by elevating him to the peerage, granting him the viscountcy."

Lord Wulverton shrugged, but there was nothing

dispassionate in the way he was staring at her, surveying her lips and her neck, then her lips again. Geneviève had thought his eyes a dull hazel before—a muddy mixture of moss and brown—but a strange light had sparked within them, making the green flicker.

The warmth that had come to her cheeks through shame seemed to grow as he looked at her, fuelled now by a different awareness—of her femininity beside his strength, and her knowledge of what had passed between them. Her knowledge of how it had felt to take him inside her.

She endeavoured to find her voice, struggling against the breath catching in her throat. "His loyalty was rewarded."

"Quite so." There were no more than a few inches between them but Lord Wulverton leaned in closer. "Some fared far worse. Wicked Lord Cavell, for instance."

"Wicked?" Geneviève licked her lips.

"Oh, yes! Fiendishly sinful! If anyone's keeping company with Satan, it's him."

"Aren't we all wicked, one way or another?" she murmured.

"One way or another, I suppose we are." His mouth brushed her hair. "As for Lord Cavell, the marriage bargain he struck brought out the very worst in him. Having wed the daughter of the man who'd sent him into financial ruin, he took his revenge on her in the most humiliating ways—accusing her of adultery with every man in their employ. Locking her in her chamber, he visited only to exercise his conjugal rights."

"She was a prisoner." The thought made Geneviève sway, but Lord Wulverton's hand was firmly behind her, resting on the small of her back.

He would kiss her, now, surely? She knew already how he would taste, and how his tongue would enter to claim her. How much she knew, and how much she remembered! She tilted her head, parting her lips in anticipation, warmth flooding her lower abdomen.

"With none for company but her loyal hound." His voice was soft and low. "In the end, she let herself down the ivy from her window and fled across the moor."

Geneviève glanced out from the window. The distance to the ground was great and the ivy, though plentiful, looked far from secure.

"And had she been unfaithful to him?" Geneviève met his eyes once more. She found his lids half closed, but the green fire within them just as bright.

"Perhaps," he replied. "Lord Cavell's actions were extreme but some would find them justifiable. No man likes to be made a fool of."

Geneviève frowned. The idea of being so controlled, losing all independence, would be unbearable to her. She made to step back, but his other hand was upon her now, at her waist, pulling her toward him.

She pushed back with both hands, anger flaring. "And no woman wishes to be denied her liberty."

As he towered over her, she saw his jaw tense and the pulse rise in his temple. He looked as if he would not just kiss her but tear the clothes from her body and consume her like a wolf hungry for its prey.

Then, just as suddenly, his expression closed, his voice becoming hard.

"Once Lord Cavell had set off in pursuit, it didn't take long for him to bring her down, and to plunge his knife into her heart."

His tone was quite poisonous, as if he were berating her for the faithlessness of Lady Cavell, and of all her sex. Shrinking back, she grasped behind her, finding the curtain's edge.

She made herself laugh, but it sounded hollow. "And what of her faithful dog? Did he not leap from the window to come to her aid?"

Lord Wulverton's lip curved but there was no playfulness in him. "It did indeed, and tore out Cavell's throat, but too late to save its mistress."

With that, he released her. Geneviève fell back against the window ledge, her knees unwilling to hold her steady.

Walking away, Lord Wulverton did not look back.

CHAPTER TEN

It had taken some time for Geneviève to compose herself. Even now, she was unsure what had occurred. She'd experienced a tilting of the world from its usual axis, and a flare of passion that had threatened to see her behave in a manner altogether contrary to that planned. Displaying her wit and charm was one thing. Allowing Lord Wulverton to seduce her, quite another.

And then…

She could barely understand it. She had said something. Done something. The change in his demeanour had been shocking, as if he ran mad. Was there mental instability in the family? It was common, she knew, in certain places remote from Society, where the pool of eligible spouses was limited. How else to explain his behavior?

Geneviève declined to attend luncheon, excusing herself with a headache, but she could hardly remain closeted forever. Her designs stood unchanged. She would encourage Hugo into a proposal, then depart the moor and return to France. It was simply a matter of keeping her head.

Hugo rose as she entered the drawing room, lifting her hand briefly to his lips before ushering her to a seat between himself and Mrs. Wapshot.

Geneviève noted that Beatrice was dressed very prettily in a skirt and jacket of navy jacquard, though her blouse perhaps bore an excess of lace. Her fair hair had been pinned most charmingly in 'Gibson Girl' style. It was simply her bad luck that Geneviève had staked her claim upon Hugo. Whatever prior attachment had been forming, Beatrice's golden innocence was no match for Geneviève's darkly feminine allure.

Hugo was all attention, inquiring after her poor head, then directing her toward the most delicious of the fancies. They were drinking spiced wine, which Hugo insisted she sample while it was hot.

From where he stood behind Lady Marguerite's chair, Lord Wulverton turned to stare at Geneviève quite blatantly. Whatever mood had possessed him before seemed to have alleviated only moderately, for the intensity of his gaze was extreme—as if to delve her soul.

Heaven forbid he should do so successfully!

The Reverend took a sip from his glass. "How blessed we are. Not all are as fortunate, gathering in festive cheer."

Marguerite raised her glass. "You're most welcome.

What merriment can there be if one lacks friends with whom to celebrate?"

Reverend Wapshot nodded, taking a mince pie from the tray. "It's at this time that I feel most for those poor souls in the prison, who have little to remind them of the joys of the season."

Hugo shifted in his seat. "Quite so, Reverend— although, of course, they are criminals, duly sentenced and punished. We could hardly expect the taxpayer to indulge them with sweetmeats and claret."

Mrs. Wapshot leaned closer to Geneviève, speaking in an undertone. "I try not to think too much of the proximity of that place, nor the nature of the men who reside there. You know there was a break out almost a month ago? Three men on the loose, having made skeleton keys out of bones from their dinner!" She puckered her lips. "If I was in charge, I'd not give them any meat at all."

Geneviève whispered in reply, as the others continued their conversation. "And one is yet to be apprehended?"

"If there's any justice, he's been taken by the moor. There was a thick mist that night, so the chances are he came to a bad end in the mire." Mrs. Wapshot's eyes were positively gleaming.

Geneviève rather hoped the poor fellow had gotten away. Perhaps some of the moor folk had seen fit to help his escape.

"One fatal step and you're thigh-deep and done for!" declared Mrs. Wapshot. "Whole sheep and ponies have been lost on these moors. Divine justice, I'd say, if the criminal was sucked down straight to Beelzebub's furnace!" She uttered the last with relish.

Geneviève recoiled at the thought of such a horrible fate. "How terrifying!"

"More terrible if we were strangled in our beds," hissed Mrs. Wapshot, looking about her as if the would-be perpetrator might be lurking behind the sofa. "Or worse! Some of those men haven't seen a woman in decades! Think on that!"

It appeared that Mrs. Wapshot had given it a great deal of consideration. The lemon fancy she raised to her lips disappeared in one ferocious bite.

Geneviève felt the pressure of Hugo's arm against hers. "Don't worry," he murmured. "You're safe here." He reached to fondle the ear of the rough-coated wolfhound at his feet. "If any brute comes near, Tootle and Muffin will show them what for."

Inching her knee away from the spindle of drool which threatened her skirts, Geneviève arranged her face in a gracious smile. As long as the ruffian appeared with a tasty titbit, she doubted they'd have much to fear. Muffin's attention was fixed solely upon the uneaten morsel on her plate.

"Of course, there's no need for you to shy from them," added Hugo. "They'd never attack anyone we presented as a guest."

Geneviève tried to return her concentration to Reverend Wapshot, who was speaking enthusiastically between mouthfuls of fruitcake.

"I visit the men every Sabbath for their sacred communion with the Lord and, whatever their misdeeds, they offer sincere devotion in that hour of supplication." The Reverend scanned the room with a satisfied air.

Lord Wulverton scowled. "Hardly surprising, when you consider how they spend the majority of their hours, entombed within the gray walls of their cells. Enough to send a man mad. Little wonder they take the opportunity to stretch their legs and their voices, nor that they make regular attempts to escape altogether."

"Quite so," agreed Reverend Wapshot, shaking his head and extending his glass to Withers's approach with the decanter. "We pray for them, don't we my dears?"

Beatrice nodded meekly, but Mrs. Wapshot jolted upright. "May they know the error of their ways and repent! The cold of their cells will seem as nothing to the searing fires of hell's damnation, to which they're destined for their heinous crimes."

Glancing at Lord Wulverton, Geneviève noted his expression of extreme distaste. Nevertheless, he said nothing. There was a clatter at his elbow, however, as Withers wobbled, almost dropping his tray.

"Steady there!" The viscount caught the butler as his knees buckled, removing the glassware from his trembling hands before mishap could occur.

"So sorry, m'lord," Withers mumbled, apparently not at all himself.

"Dash it, Withers, you're not well!" pronounced Hugo, leaping to support his other side. "Come along. We'll get you to your parlor and Mrs. Fuddleby will make you a reviving pot of tea."

Tootle, who'd positioned himself hopefully, at Mrs.

Wapshot's side, lumbered off as the door opened. Though the spot had been advantageous in the way of pastry crumbs, the dog clearly wasn't fond of raised voices. The kitchen hearth would be infinitely more restful.

"Ours is a forgiving God, my love," the Reverend softly chided. "And it's our duty, here on earth, to show the same mercy. We're all less than perfect, are we not?"

Mrs. Wapshot appeared to have a ready retort but a stern look from her husband, combined with Betsy's arrival with a tray of jam tarts, diverted her from further proclamation.

There was a short silence, broken only by the clatter of forks upon plates and the sipping of wine. Muffin gave a great sigh and shuffled round to lay his head in Marguerite's lap.

At last, Beatrice spoke, having barely said a word for the most part. "Everyone deserves a second chance. Whatever our human weaknesses, we can learn to rise above them."

"Hear, hear!" agreed Geneviève, giving Beatrice a smile of encouragement.

"What have I missed?" asked Hugo, returning as the conversation became easy once more, this time on the merits of blackberry wine over damson.

"Reverend Wapshot is inviting you to the rectory tomorrow to sample his homemade wines, Hugo," said Marguerite. "Perhaps, our dear comtesse may like to join you."

Mrs. Wapshot pursed her lips, but before any more

could be said, Lord Wulverton interrupted, having reappeared in the doorway.

"I need an extra pair of hands with me to visit the tenants. The countess may like to see how the moorland farming folk live, and the importance of our benevolent traditions." He glowered at the back of Mrs. Wapshot's head. "I've a dozen geese to deliver, and Mrs. Fuddleby is making up baskets of preserves and pickles."

All this he'd uttered without looking at Geneviève, but he turned to her now, his eyes piercing, as if defying her to make some excuse.

"I could help," piped up Hugo, "In the car, you know."

Lord Wulverton waved his hand dismissively. "Hardly built for rutted farm tracks is it, that machine of yours, and no room to put the baskets either. Far easier with the trap and pair."

Hugo conceded with a sniff. Meanwhile, Marguerite looked as if a vat of soured milk had just been placed under her nose.

"All settled then." Viscount Wulverton might have been absent from his ancestral home for more than two decades, but he appeared to be having no difficulty stepping into his role as Master of the Moor.

Maxim had been old enough to be Geneviève's grandfather, give or take a few years. The viscount, at a pinch, could have sired her. Hugo was more akin to a little brother. Putting aside the volatility of his moods, there was no doubt that Lord Wulverton would make the more engaging husband of the two, despite the irrational outburst she'd witnessed that morning. However, it was Hugo she needed to win over if she was to return to Château Rosseline with her head held high.

She wondered if the viscount had somehow gotten the measure of her and, if so, what he might propose to do about it. Had he sensed her plan to entice Hugo and was intervening to thwart her, or was his interest more self-serving?

She was aware of his passionate nature, and the attraction between them was surely mutual. It had been that, she surmised, which had inspired the bizarre fit of temper she'd witnessed. He had fought to control his animal urges, and the result had been a show of force. How like a man to blame his own lack of control on a woman's wiles, as if the desire that had flared between them had been a re-enactment of Adam's temptation.

Even so, perhaps he intended to drive her to some remote track and initiate a more thorough seduction.

Such an overture would create the worst of complications, yet Geneviève's stomach fluttered at the thought.

CHAPTER ELEVEN

SHE HAD KEPT HIM WAITING. As she descended the steps, Lord Wulverton was blowing on his hands and foot stamping. When he turned, looking at her with those piercing green eyes, and offering his hand to help her into the cart, she hesitated.

Several times, in the night, she'd woken. Her dreams were always vivid, and they were currently stoked with an alarming degree of fuel. She had imagined every sort of scenario from the coming day but, each time, had ended with the same conclusion. Geneviève blushed to think of it.

Lord Wulverton was clearly not quite a gentleman. Rather, he was just the sort of gentleman that appealed to Geneviève's baser nature. Accompanying him today was madness, and she might have invented any sort of excuse to avoid the outing. But she had not.

Whatever transpires, I must keep my head, she reminded herself, allowing him to settle her on the sprung seat and place a woollen rug about her legs.

She had wondered if he would make an apology for his snappish behavior, and the near-violence he had shown her. However, he made no reference to what had passed.

To begin with, neither spoke as the wheels of the cart creaked over the frost-hardened ground. Lord Wulverton merely nodded to indicate what he thought might be of interest within the undulating landscape, a fox stalking silently ahead, its eyes on some smaller creature unseen, and a rough circle of stones with a buzzard circling above. Cottages huddled beneath the hills, slated roofs yellowed with lichen, lowering over walls thick as castle keeps, others roughly thatched.

Geneviève's cheeks were numb from the chill, though the sun's strength prevented her from feeling too cold. Wearing her thickest clothing and keeping the rug firmly tucked about her, she was surprisingly comfortable.

There was little enough room upon the seat of the cart. The length of the viscount's legs compelled him to sit with them parted, holding the reins between. It was impossible for her to avoid her leg touching his, while each bump over the dry-rutted mud brought them together with a jolt.

After some few hundred yards, she set aside propriety, slightly leaning into him and allowing her hip to nestle his. In this way, they swayed as one. Twice, the cart lurched so violently that she was forced to steady herself by placing her hand on his thigh. However, not once did his hands stray from their job in directing the horses, nor did he touch her in any way that could be interpreted as intentional.

Nevertheless, she felt certain that he took pleasure in the rocking motion which drew them together. Despite the many layers of clothing between them, she was aware of his body—its warmth and hardness, while the soft curve of her breast pressed somewhere above the crook of his elbow.

As they reached the top of the first track, chickens scattered, and Geneviève caught the rich smell of a peat fire, its smoke carried on the crisp morning air, overlaying the scent of sheep's dung and urine and rotting vegetation.

A black-faced sheepdog missing a rear leg ambled out to greet them, followed by the lady of the house, who dipped a curtsey.

Geneviève stayed in the cart as Lord Wulverton swung down, greeting the woman and tugging at the ears of the two children peeking from behind her skirts.

The woman drew off her apron, patting her hair. "It's so cold—like as not to snow afore Christmas, and here ye are comin' out to see us! Yer a sight for sore eyes, Master, and that's no doubt."

She spoke with a great deal of familiarity, touching the viscount's arm and speaking to him more as the boy she remembered from years past than as the lord of all that could be seen from one horizon to the next.

"Shame it be that old Jim b'aint here to see ye back from foreign parts. Him all'un did say ye'd be back, an' him were right."

She dabbed at her eye with the corner of the apron as Lord Wulverton lifted down the basket intended for her family, and insisted on them taking a mug of warmed milk before they departed. Geneviève would have refused but for the viscount accepting. As it was, she surreptitiously wiped the edge of her cup before drinking.

It was the same at each place they visited. Often, ale or broth were fetched, and the best wishes given for the season.

On such short acquaintance, Geneviève would not have presumed to say she knew Lord Wulverton. In fact, with each passing hour, she felt as though he became more of an enigma. Today, she'd seen another side to him—one without arrogance or condescension, or any sign of temper. He was another man entirely.

However, at their final stop, the jovial greetings were tempered by more sombre talk—of the convict, still loose. Geneviève heard only part of the exchange, and the Devon accent was hard for her to follow.

"God help ee!" said one. "They'um do escape more often at this time o' year, yearnin' fer theys' loved uns and not bein' able t' bear the thought o' spending Christmas in that place."

"They'um'll find the corpse i' the spring, I reckon," said another. "When they hikers from Exeter and the like come fer exploring."

Geneviève shivered at the thought. Was the convict even now curled in some hollow beneath the crags, too weak to walk any further, or had he eluded capture purely by dint of having already died of exposure?

Lord Wulverton was grim-faced when he climbed back upon the cart.

"Have none seen him?" Geneviève asked. "Might any moor-dweller have given shelter? Though he's a wanted man and a stranger, would they have helped?"

"He's no stranger," said Wulverton. "His name's Silas."

"You know of him?" Geneviève saw how pale the viscount looked, taking up the reins again to lead them from the farmyard and back down the muddy track.

"More than that. He was our stableman, years ago. The first to put me on a horse, before I could walk."

"But how did he come to be in prison? If he was of good character, wouldn't your father have spoken for him?"

Lord Wulverton barked a hollow sound, a muscle working at the side of his jaw. "It was he who sent him there! I didn't know, of course, until years later. My father held the magistrate in his pocket. None would have dared gone against him. It was one of the reasons I chose to join my regiment when I was old enough to make my own choices."

"You became estranged over his treatment of your stableman?" Geneviève wasn't sure she understood.

The viscount's brow knitted. "Not quite, but there's no point in talking of it now. I'd meant to visit him before the year was out and see what could be done. It was one of the tasks I'd set for myself—one of the burdens on my ledger."

"Imprisoned all this time?" Geneviève caught his

grimace and a passing flash of pain in his eyes before his face closed again.

"As with many things, I've waited too long, and now the chance is past. God knows if he's still alive."

They rode in silence to the main road, Geneviève sensing that it would be better not to speak. If Wulverton had more to say, he'd confide in his own time. His family history was no business of hers, although she supposed it would be, once she and Hugo were wedded.

After some minutes, they came to a crossroads and she recognized what lay to the north-eastward path, a web of tangled oak, bent from exposure to the bleak winds, twisted and festooned with ivy and creeping plants. The last time she'd passed this way had been at night. Now, she saw that the trunks and low-spread branches were thick-covered in velvet moss, emitting the moist, nutty aroma of ancient wood. So densely did they grow that it seemed impossible to envision what creatures might live within, other than those of nightmarish imagination.

What light would penetrate? Only animals that sought dark places would abide there—those who snuffled for their meal without need for sight.

Wistman's Wood, Hugo had called it—a place favored by Satan. With the afternoon light fading, Geneviève could see how such tales would take hold. Was the convict here, perhaps, deep inside this place that few dared enter?

A streak of cinnamon flashed before the cart, diving across the bracken. The surprise of it caused

Geneviève to catch her breath, clutching at Lord Wulverton's arm.

"Nothing to worry us," he said, releasing one hand from the reins to place over her own—a hand reassuringly large and warm. "Just a red fox running for the woods."

With relief, she saw it was true—that its brush was disappearing into the dusk and the trees. Despite his sudden changes of mood and the clouds that seemed to brood over him, having Wulverton next to her, so very much in control, made her feel safe.

Naturally, her cap remained set at Hugo; she'd exerted far too much effort on that score to abandon her plan. Yet, it was Wulverton she wished to know better and for him to see her pleasure in his company. Earlier in the day, she'd been concerned about the damp and cold, and the inadequacy of her cloak and boots. Now, she was sorry the journey would soon come to an end.

She searched for the right tone of conversation, wanting him to know that she was moved by his depth of feeling for the moor. "You fit comfortably here," she said at last. "Among the people, I mean." She wasn't sure quite how to phrase what she wished to say. "They have a love for you. It must be gratifying, after being away so long. They respect you, and you're glad to be back, I think."

He didn't answer at once, his concentration upon turning the cart at the crossroads, from where he took the southern path. When he spoke it was with quiet earnestness. "I admire them—for their affinity with the hills and rocks and mires. They're solitary and hard-working in a place largely inhospitable. I admire their resilience, and their allegiance to one another. There are none like them, at least not as I've found in my travels through the world."

As he spoke, she thought again how ruggedly handsome he was, with his own resilience and sense of allegiance. Having watched him with the moorlanders, she saw that he'd be a good master, treating them as men and women deserved—equal in God's eyes and his own.

Her impulse was to lean close and breathe his masculine scent, to bring herself so near that it would be impossible for him to avoid kissing her. There was no one to see them. She would let him. She wanted him to. Her mouth grew dry thinking of it.

He made no overture toward her, however, and she chided herself for wishing it.

The boulders of the curving moor had turned granite-black against the darkening sky and the winter-gray expanse. The fading of the light and Lord Wulverton's closeness within the cart seemed to encourage the sharing of confidences, for he continued.

"All the time I was in foreign lands, I kept thinking I'd die and be buried in the dust, far away. When my time comes, I want to be placed here, beneath the racing sky and the wind breathing through the grass, under the cold peat and moss, with the tors keeping watch over me."

She nodded. Whatever his past, he belonged on the moor.

Geneviève realized that she hadn't thought of her

own home for many hours. Instead, she'd been consumed by the landscape through which they'd travelled, and consumed by watching him.

"And what of you?" he asked. "I imagine something more than the desire to become better acquainted with your sister-in-law has brought you here."

Suppressing a tremble of alarm, she kept her eyes upon his hands, guiding the horses. It was a rare occasion when Geneviève told an unadulterated truth. Complete honesty was generally unnecessary. Dangerous even. He didn't need to hear the sordid details of her past, but she felt inclined to give him something that wasn't wholly a lie.

"I don't like to be reliant on others, but it would suit me to marry again, for the status it affords."

She seldom mentioned her fears. Steely determination was more her style. Nevertheless, she permitted Wulverton a glimpse at what she preferred to keep hidden. "The modest circumstances of my past are a hindrance in finding a husband among my former acquaintances. At least any husband I'd consider suitable."

She saw no judgement in his expression and it emboldened her to continue. "I came with the expectation of Marguerite introducing me to her own Society."

His lips twitched. "And how is that proceeding?"

"I find I must congratulate Mrs. Wapshot and Mrs. Hissop on having claimed the most eligible bachelors!"

He laughed at that.

"You were raised in a convent, I hear. An austere upbringing, I imagine."

"The nuns were kind, though no more than you might expect."

He betrayed no distaste, but Geneviève was reluctant to share too many particulars. "The hardest part was knowing my mother had given me up. I was too young to understand why she'd done so. Even now, I fail to fully comprehend how she could have left me..." Her throat grew constricted.

He made no move to comfort her—did not touch her or offer any platitude of sympathy. Instead, he merely nodded. "I was barely four years old when I lost my own mother, and only seven when my father sent me away to school."

Such things were common among the British nobility—sending boy children away to grow into men. She'd vowed that, if she ever had a child of her own, she'd keep them with her for as long as possible. There were other ways to show children how to be strong and brave than to take them from loving arms and oblige them to fend for themselves.

It was a discussion for another time. For now, she sensed enough had been shared. Better to speak of something else.

A mist had been tumbling over the bare masses of stone standing jagged above them, easing down the side of the hill. It wouldn't be long before it reached the road.

Geneviève made efforts to lighten the mood. "Dr. Hissop told me about the piskies sending the mists to confuse us. I hope your horses know their way back."

"They're only low clouds." Lord Wulverton peered

up to where she was looking. "We're a thousand feet above the rest of the county here. Clouds need stoop very little to embrace the moor."

"You've the soul of a poet!" Geneviève mused, inspiring another of his half smiles.

They'd almost reached the hall, though not by its grand gates and the avenue. He had taken them behind, approaching via the smaller track which led past the chapel, to the rear of the hall. The frost was creeping through the verge on either side.

"I'll be back before you know it." He brought the horses to a standstill. "It's bitter out here, but I should visit my father's grave and that of my brother. My mother's, too. I've a shameful habit of putting aside what discomfits me."

He touched her shoulder. "Thank you for your company today."

Swinging down, he headed through the lychgate, in search of the newest headstones among those of his ancestors, held within the walls of the small patch of sacred ground. Geneviève wrapped her cloak tighter and peered after him, watching for his return.

Geneviève knew what it was to be alone and preferred to find her own way. She'd been sure of her plan in coming to England, knowing what she must do. However, in these last hours, it had felt as if her path were shrouded and what she needed to see was just out of sight.

As she sat, the air seemed to grow thicker and all about her gloomier, the uncertain moon straining through the mist.

She jumped as a woodcock burst from a patch of fern, fleeing startled. Someone was near—brushing through the grass, but not from the direction of the graveyard. From the other side, perhaps.

"Lord Wulverton?" The fog muffled her cry, so that she wondered if she'd uttered it aloud or only in her mind. "Who's there?"

When she saw him, it was so fleetingly that she wondered if he were a man at all—so haunted was his face and hollow-eyed.

"Withers?"

He'd looked at her but a moment before disappearing into the gloom. Now, she saw only drifting mist and shifting shadows. 'Piskie-led' Dr. Hissop had called it, the trance which overtook the unwary until they knew not what was real and what of their imagination. He'd told her one should turn one's coat or cape inside out to break their mischievous spell. Ridiculous! As if she would!

Except that she was not alone, for the horses were fidgeting in their harness, sensing something near.

She heard the panting first and the rush of bounding feet before she saw the glint of eyes—not one creature but two, or were there more? They were moving low and from her right, from the direction of the hall.

What had Hugo called them? Wisht Hounds? They were creatures born of ignorant superstition, she knew, but all such stories had some footprint in the truth. Conan Doyle believed so, too, didn't he? She'd begun reading the book Mallon had lent her—of the curse of *The Hound of the Baskervilles.* That was just a story though, written to thrill and entertain. Besides which, she'd committed no sin worthy of attracting other-worldly retribution, had she?

As the first howl rent the air, Geneviève let forth a scream of her own.

CHAPTER TWELVE

IT TOOK but a few minutes for Lord Wulverton to bring them down from the chapel, driving directly to the servants' entrance. Geneviève remembered little beyond waking beside the cart, her face wet from the drizzling mist. Had she fainted? She'd felt cold to the bone but how wonderful it had been to feel his strong arms about her, lifting her gently into the back of the cart.

"She needs warming, Mrs. Fuddleby," he announced, carrying Geneviève into the kitchen.

"Sit 'er ladyship in my armchair an we'll stoke up them flames." The cook showed little surprise at her master's abrupt entrance into her domain.

He did just that before taking the wooden stool on the other side, pulling off his gloves and then Geneviève's. Taking her hands in his, he rubbed them vigorously.

Mrs. Fuddleby lifted down a saucepan. "Hot milk and nutmeg's what's needed—like when yer were a little 'un, eh Master."

He seemed to know his way around, going out to the passageway beyond the kitchen and returning with a blanket, placing it over Geneviève's knees.

"Like old times, bain't it," said the cook, taking up the grater for her nutmeg. "Nummer o' times yer sat there as a boy, come to 'ave yer knee bandaged or yer heart comforted." She beamed fondly, taking stock of the hulking man perched upon the stool. "Yer've grown a mite since, I do say."

"A little, yes." He smiled.

They sat companionably for some minutes, listening to the spit and hiss of the burning logs, and Mrs. Fuddleby's efficient bustle. Geneviève felt very safe. Her earlier attack of fright hadn't been like her at all.

Nevertheless, she felt compelled to ask. Had he heard what she had done? Had he seen those eyes staring through the mist?

"A howl, you say?" Wulverton looked thoughtful. "No, nothing like that, though the mist does have a way of altering sound. A wild dog, maybe. There are some, scavenging on the moor."

"It's most likely my imagination. I've been hearing too many of your legends and have furnished my own spectral hounds." She really was feeling far more herself, and sufficiently warmed to remove her cloak.

"There yer go, my lovelies," said Mrs. Fuddleby, doing away with all formality. "And be sure to drink it down while it's got a bit o' steam." She nodded approvingly as Geneviève sipped from her cup.

Wulverton swigged from his, then took leave of Mrs.

Fuddleby with a kiss to her forehead. Nodding to Geneviève, in four great strides, he was out of the door through which they'd entered, returning to the horses waiting patiently.

Mrs. Fuddleby followed the sight of him until the door had shut and gave a sigh. At the kitchen table, she began cracking eggs, separating the whites. Geneviève watched as the cook's strong right arm commenced whisking.

"You're very fond of him," said Geneviève.

"That I am. I can scarce believe the master be back at Wulverton." She sniffed. "There's no better piece o' joy."

"I can see he holds affection for you, too." Geneviève unpinned the shawl from her neck.

"I should say so!" declared Mrs. Fuddleby, tossing her head, although she looked gratified at Geneviève's comment. "I had the raisin' of 'im for long enough. Even when the mistress were with us, her never did spend much time with Master Mallon, nor little Edward. He were only a baby when she did leave the two mites."

Geneviève noted the cook's use of Lord Wulverton's given name. She'd known him from his babyhood, of course.

"He mentioned her to me, just a little," Geneviève replied.

Mrs. Fuddleby pursed her lips. "A terrible shock it were, what did 'appen, although some might say it were a blessin'. Certain folks never do be satisfied in this mortal life."

Geneviève rather fell into that camp herself. Acquiring a state of contentment was no easy task.

"She were a great beauty, yer know." Mrs. Fuddlby paused from whipping, upturning the bowl to check on the firmness. "Toast of Lunnun folks said. She weren't never goin' to be 'appy down 'ere on the moor." The cook took a forcing bag and began spooning in the meringue mixture. "Not that it were all 'er ladyship's fault. The late Viscount, God rest his soul, were no easy man to please."

"And there was some difference in their ages, I suppose."

"True enough, though that's not always a bad thing for marriage." Mrs. Fuddleby gave Geneviève something between a wink and nod.

"Still, no use cryin' over spilt milk, is it! They were both guilty o' badness and now they be inside the pearly gates. It be God they'ums must face afore they find their everlastin' peace."

Mrs. Fuddleby bent earnestly to piping her meringues. There were several things Geneviève was eager to ask but it was beneath her to encourage gossip —and the cook seemed to have said all she wished to on the matter. Nevertheless, as Geneviève made her way upstairs, she couldn't help but speculate.

MALLON POURED HIMSELF A LARGE WHISKY, gulping it down in three mouthfuls, relishing the burn in the back of his throat. He poured another, then took the decanter to the armchair closest to the fire.

Hunching low, he rested his booted foot against the

fender's edge. Stupid of him to have kept her out so long. She wasn't accustomed to the moorland's strain of winter damp. He'd suggest she stay inside for a few days. God forbid she came down with pneumonia.

His motives in having her accompany him had been selfish. He'd no intention of wooing her, or any woman, yet he'd chosen the cart, knowing its seat to be too small to accommodate the pair of them. It hadn't taken long for her to lean into him—just as he'd hoped.

And hell only knew what had come over him the previous morning, while he'd been telling her the legend of old Cavell. He'd behaved abominably, and with the barest restraint, letting her inflame him with those violet eyes and the rise and fall of what lay so temptingly within her corset. He couldn't remember the last time a woman had produced such an effect on him.

Well, that wasn't strictly true, but the occasion in question had been an aberration, and the woman on the train quite a different kettle of fish.

What had he been thinking? If he was honest, he knew damn well. The countess had been willing enough, that was for sure, but it was just as well he'd resisted. She wanted another husband, not a dalliance— and he had no intention of falling into the trap of marriage.

With his mother's example before him, how could he ever pronounce the vows between man and wife?

Still, he'd had the devil's own job not to take the countess in his arms and kiss those sensual, upturned lips. Not just yesterday, but today, in the cart. He found her physically attractive, of course, but she was also sensitive and thoughtful—and with a brain in her head when she'd a mind to use it.

What had it been like between his parents? Had his father chosen his mother for her looks alone? She'd brought only a modest dowry. Her beauty must have been her fortune, though little good it had done her. Not a single portrait remained of his mother in the hall. Generations of de Wolfes populated the long gallery, but she was not among them. Mallon remembered her from memory alone, with an expression of wistful sadness on her face, more often than not.

He'd no plans to repeat the travesty of his parents' union. He'd had plenty of women, but he'd paid them to perform services. Nothing more.

It was the best way, unless a man wanted an heir.

Some simple local woman might make an adequate companion, he supposed, and would bear him sturdy little tykes. Such a woman might be content to remain here, on the moor. However, among the type of female he generally found attractive, he couldn't imagine any being satisfied with the lack of sophistication or their remote location. Even the drive to Exeter and back required a full day.

Moreover, Mallon didn't need a nursery of brats. It was enough for him to call the moor home again and to continue his ancestral traditions, then allow Hugo to inherit the Wulverton title and estate. Though Hugo had inherited the Rosseline vineyards, Mallon could hardly imagine his nephew taking up permanent residence there.

Mallon had been nonchalant when the telegram had first arrived at his barracks, letting him know that his brother had taken a wife. Better him than me, Mallon had thought. Later, he heard how his father had crossed the Channel to restock his cellar and had returned with the only daughter of Count Rosseline. Marguerite's father had bestowed a dowry large enough to repair the roof of Wulverton Hall five times over, not to mention a thousand bottles of the finest burgundy—all in return for marrying into one of England's oldest families.

Whatever fondness Mallon had felt for his father, it had died for want of nurture. From the day of his mother's departure, the old man's heart had turned against his sons. Perhaps he'd doubted their blood was his, or looking at them had reminded him too much of their mother. The outcome was the same, in either case.

Ironic, of course, that he and Edward had been born with the customary dark hair and green eyes of the de Wolfes, while his father had been sandy haired. Perhaps, that was where Hugo's extreme blondness hailed from, if not from Marguerite.

It had been a relief for Mallon to escape. Leaving Edward had been a wrench but he'd been a young man of eighteen by then — old enough to look out for himself.

Mallon had never intended to return. But, as the

years went by, his yearning for the moor had only grown. So, here he was.

It was regrettable that his arrival coincided with the festive season, and an inevitable stream of guests, but he would do his best to endure. There would be time enough for solitude when the new year began.

CHAPTER THIRTEEN

When Marguerite entered, Lisette was placing a gold-plumed aigrette into Geneviève's hair.

"How pretty you look, my dear." Marguerite took in the dark copper evening gown in heavy damask, its neckline sweeping low across Geneviève's shoulders. For a woman neither born of aristocratic blood nor raised in a noble household, she carried the trappings well.

"You may leave us, Lisette." Geneviève dismissed her maid.

Contemplating her guest through the mirror's reflection, Marguerite saw that Geneviève wore the Rosseline diamonds—drop earrings, a three-stranded bracelet, and a delicate choker. Three centuries of jewels had passed to Maxim on their mother's death. All were now in this young woman's possession, according to the provision of his will. Only on Geneviève's death would their ownership revert to Maxim's heir. Marguerite herself had received little more than a string of her mother's pearls and a matching bracelet, the clasp of which had an annoying habit of coming loose.

With my plans coming to fruition, the injustice of the legacy will soon be remedied. Marrying the comtesse, Hugo will regain control of everything. In deportment, I cannot fault her, and she's young enough to bear the necessary number of children.

Marguerite had been in the world long enough to recognize a woman's coquetry. Geneviève appeared to be as keen on the union as she. This being the case, the issue would soon be settled.

There were no obstacles to the arrangement as far as Marguerite could see, bar the complication of Mallon's return. It hadn't escaped her notice that the new viscount had been displaying interest in their guest.

The sooner they announced an engagement the better. It really wouldn't do to have him lure her to his bed, or for the hussy to decide in favor of the immediate title of Viscountess Wulverton.

"And how well our family jewels suit you." Marguerite placed her hand upon Geneviève's shoulder, composing an expression of benevolent admiration.

"You're too kind," said Geneviève. "I thought Hugo might like to see me wear them." She lowered her lashes in coy modesty.

Marguerite resisted the temptation to roll her eyes. The time had surely passed for playacting. They were both aware of the other's hand.

"Perfectly true. My son may be young but he has excellent taste."

Geneviève looked up at Marguerite. "And he's well-guided by those who have his best interests at heart."

"Quite so." Marguerite smiled. Bestowed with only one child, it was fortunate that she'd produced a boy. However, a daughter would have been such a comfort. After they'd moved to the château, she and Geneviève would be thrown a great deal into each other's company. It was not an unpleasant prospect.

"To speak plainly, my dear, I've come to give you my blessing." Marguerite moved to sit upon the chest at the end of Geneviève's bed. "As Hugo's mother, I know something of his nature, and his heart, and I see that you'd make a suitable wife. I need not enumerate the reasons. As you see, I hide nothing and encourage us to be candid with one another. In short, I approve the match."

Geneviève's eyes were alight with interest. "Honesty is always desirable—since it saves so much time—and I see we're of one mind." She appeared to consider how to phrase her next statement. "Hugo's attentions are welcome to me but they require encouragement. He's almost too gentlemanly, I fear."

Marguerite waved her hand imperiously. "In such a case, it's up to us to exert our powers of persuasion. Yours, I've no doubt, are adequate to the task. Tonight's gathering may provide the opportunity, if you wish not to delay."

She rose, taking some steps to leave. It hadn't been her intention to mention Mallon, but Marguerite turned back toward Geneviève. "Of course, it would be naïve of us to imagine that you have no other…choices, before you. It may amuse the viscount, for instance, to pay you some attention, and a man's flattery can be just as inducing as our own."

Geneviève seemed to sit up a little straighter.

"I wish only to warn you." Marguerite rested her hand upon the handle of the door. "We cannot know the extent to which his past is littered with…unsavoury behaviors, but we may surmise…" It was vexing to skirt around the obvious, but some things even Marguerite could not bring herself to spell out. God only knew what vices Mallon had indulged, living so long in unciv-ilized lands.

"Such men are not always to be relied upon, and I'd hate to see you lose your head." She smiled tightly. "Or your heart, to one who might easily come to disregard it."

CHAPTER FOURTEEN

IT HAD BEEN a long time since Mallon had been obliged to endure the company of so many. He'd never been keen on formality, nor conversation with those he hardly knew, but it was ridiculous to let nerves get the better of him. He was preparing for a dinner at which twenty would be seated, followed by a little music and a few waltzes. It was hardly the storming of the battlefield with cannons blazing.

All that was needed was the appearance of confidence. He was master of Wulverton Hall, Viscount Wulverton. Men would part before him, while the women would observe with that particular form of awareness with which he was familiar. It had been so even before he assumed the title.

He would have to suffer tedious small talk. He might recount any trifling anecdote, and the company would be amused, but it bored him to indulge the wits of those whose brains were only lightly filled.

It was an evening to be endured rather than holding

any expectation of pleasure and yet there was one person he wished to seek out.

He located her, at last, on the far side of the room, or heard her rather—for her laughter was unmistakable, husky and sensual. His stomach knotted in response and a swell rose in his heart—a strange tugging sensation that urged him closer, drawing him toward her.

Even from behind, he knew her at once. No other woman in the room had so elegant a neck nor hair so luxuriant. She appeared to have recovered from her fright, and from being chilled, with no ill-effects.

Under the chandelier's candlelight, her gown appeared to shimmer. Meanwhile, the diamonds at her ears and neck were obscenely large. If they were real, she was undoubtedly better provided for than he'd realized.

Making his way closer, he saw that she was engaged in speaking to Hugo and to someone Mallon didn't recognize—a tall fellow with a supercilious air. He'd seen enough of that kind during his army days. Young men with little to recommend them in the way of talent or virtue; men whose egos were fed purely by the blueness of their blood.

This one seemed to be having trouble deciding which part of the countess to devour first—her décolleté or her jewels.

"Damned backwater if you ask me. Don't know how you stand it."

Mallon caught the drift of the conversation from several feet away. The impertinent cur also appeared to have taken a surfeit of liquor, for his words were slurred.

"Steady on, Slagsby. It's not as bad as all that."

Hugo's remonstrations were having not the slightest effect.

"I expect our lovely countess feels the same." The toad was leaning indecently against her arm.

"Not at all!" Her voice was crystal. She was turning away, attempting to place some inches between them.

"No need to sugar coat it for young de Wolfe's benefit!" The churl slapped Hugo on the back, then slung his arm about Hugo's neck, his gaze now fixed on the upper curve of Geneviève's breasts and his voice rising. "We used to share everything at school, didn't we Wolfers. No secrets here. We like to deliver it straight up, eh!" He gave a lecherous wink and guffawed at his wit, causing several other guests to swivel their heads in disapproval.

"We'd best get some food inside you, old chum. 'Bout time Withers rang the gong." Hugo staggered under his friend's arm.

"Or to bed, I'd say." Mallon drew alongside.

"Ha! Not without my dinner, and I was planning on sitting next to this pretty piece. Two ripe fruits to finish with, eh!" Slagsby's knees suddenly failed him, obliging Mallon and Hugo to take his full weight.

"Dash it, Slagsby. You're a disgrace!" Hugo shot Geneviève a look of abject embarrassment.

The color had risen on her cheeks but she held her poise. Mallon, meanwhile, felt decidedly less composed. The chatter in the room had disguised most of Slagsby's uncouth comments, but the Reverend Wapshot and his wife had most certainly had an earful.

Under other circumstances, he'd take the oaf outside for a good thrashing. As it was, a subtler approach was required. With a nod to Hugo, Mallon hoisted up Lord Slagsby and, ignoring his protests, removed him swiftly.

"VERY DECENT OF YOU. Don't know what got into him, although he always was a trifle boisterous—at school, you know." Hugo dabbed at his forehead with his handkerchief. Slagsby had passed out halfway up the stairs, turning into a deadweight. It had taken enormous effort to drag him to his bed.

"Not your fault, Hugo. Though you might want to reassess your friendship." Mallon did his best to keep his temper.

His own opinion of Lord Slagsby remained unwavering. The man was an ill-mannered, lecherous drunk and a gambler; removing his jacket, a handful of betting slips had fluttered to the floor. Mallon feared Hugo was too impressionable. Men like Slagsby tainted everything they touched. Hugo appeared a decent young man, but he was green enough to be led astray. Mallon knew that path and was in no hurry to see his nephew make similar mistakes.

Another duty I've been remiss in fulfilling. Mallon knew he owed it to his brother to have a care for his only son. *I might have no hope of happiness in a woman's arms but I'll do my best to see Hugo well-settled.*

Returning downstairs, they were ushered immediately into the dining room, Marguerite directing Mallon to lead in both Reverend Wapshot's elderly mother and aunt, while Hugo offered his arm to the countess.

The meal was interminable. Seated at the head of the table and flanked on either side, Mallon had little choice but to apply himself to the courtesies of dinner-talk, but it was no easy task. Both ladies were hard of hearing and had interest only in the food before them.

His gaze wandered to the opposite end, where Hugo held court, Geneviève to his right and his mother upon his left. There, the conversation appeared to be flowing in a lively manner. How had he not seen it before? There was an attraction between them. The countess had touched his arm five times in as many minutes while Hugo was hardly eating at all, his attention all upon his fair companion.

Marguerite, he noted, looked well contented. The countess was Hugo's senior by perhaps seven years. Not the norm by any stretch of the imagination. It was a curious piece of matchmaking, but he'd seen stranger.

Mallon chewed upon a forkful of trout. He'd initially thought the sauce not at all bad, but it appeared flavorless now. He made an effort to swallow and took a mouthful of wine. Even that—a fine vintage he'd chosen himself from the well-stocked cellar—had lost its zest.

It was a relief, at last, for Marguerite to call them through to the salon, which had been cleared for dancing.

"Cigars and port will be available in the anteroom,

but no gentleman is to partake until he's had a turn-about the room to the satisfaction of our ladies." She rose from her seat, ushering her guests.

"Beatrice, you'll play the piano for us? Perhaps a waltz? And Hugo should lead us in the merriment, with the comtesse, I think."

The Wapshots' daughter looked plaintively at Hugo as she took her seat at the instrument. Holding a torch for his nephew, most certainly. Regrettable that she wasn't from a more notable family. Not that such things mattered particularly. Whatever a woman's birth, romantic love was an illusion—a temporary madness soon replaced by tedium.

Mallon's attention was brought back by Marguerite's chiding. "Partners are needed, Lord Wulverton."

Across the room, both Mrs. Hissop and Mrs. Wapshot looked hopeful. The thought of partnering them held no allure but he could hardly refuse. As he advanced, Mrs. Wapshot, resplendent in apricot taffeta, darted forward. "Such a pleasure, your Lordship." She seized his arm, propelling him to join the other couples.

It had been many years since Mallon had danced formally, or attended a festive occasion come to that. Mrs. Wapshot was lacking lightness of foot and rather too inclined to lead, but Mallon was, at least, spared the necessity of looking at her. Over her head, he was able to direct his gaze to what most interested him.

Hugo and Geneviève made a handsome pair, moving gracefully to the majestic strains of Strauss, his hand lightly upon her waist, guiding her through the center of the room. Hardly surprising that Hugo was smitten. The countess was not only ravishing but seemed to have eyes only for her partner, laughing still, bestowing all her charm.

A tightness began to grip Mallon's chest followed by a surge of heat. *Anxiety?* He'd told himself that he wanted the best for Hugo. Despite the disparity in their ages, there was no reason why Geneviève shouldn't prove a reasonable match. Why then, did he not feel happier?

Before arriving at the hall, his thoughts had turned repeatedly to the passionate stranger on the train. Only since meeting the countess had his mind been diverted. It was she, now, who commanded his thoughts, even away from those lustful remembrances.

The final strains closing, each couple parted. Mallon bowed his thanks to Mrs. Wapshot. The young pair had drifted to the holly-and-ivy-swathed window. Above, hanging from a hook placed for the purpose, was a large bunch of mistletoe. The countess raised her face to Hugo, whispering something.

Mallon was unable to look away as Hugo took her in his arms. She folded, softly, into him, parting her lips to receive his kiss.

The heat was not anxiety but jealousy, tinged with desire.

"Another if you would, Beatrice," called Lady Marguerite from the far side of the salon. "We cannot yet allow our gentlemen to rest."

As their kiss ended, Hugo directed the countess back to the floor. Without thinking, Mallon stepped forward.

The craving to take her in his arms was a fever beneath his skin—impossible to ignore.

"If I may?" He was already offering his hand, his eyes turning from Hugo to Geneviève.

"Of course, Uncle, of course. Splendid idea."

Hugo was mumbling something else, but Mallon was no longer paying attention. Geneviève appeared expectant—surprised but not displeased. Bowing, he led her into the dance.

He saw only her as they glided through the salon— her face looking up at him with those startling eyes, her lips so full and inviting. He pulled her tighter, his hand inching toward the back of her waist until there was barely an inch between them. He needed to bring her closer, to pull her into an embrace which would end with his mouth on hers.

She smelt of orchids, her scent carried to him by the warmth of her body. Something about that fragrance, about the sight of her bare shoulders and the swell of her breasts, was perplexing.

Suddenly, the room swam out of focus, his blood rising to roar in his ears. The walls were closing in, making it difficult for him to breathe. Sweat was beading on his back.

Releasing her, he spoke some apology. He bumped into another couple but did not turn to see. He needed air.

It was cooler in the hall but still his collar felt too tight and his heart was pounding. Wrenching open the main door, he staggered out, pulling the night into his lungs, willing his pulse to steady.

The sky was clear, the moon throwing light upon the valley before the house, and illuminating the looming hillsides beyond. It was too cold for him to stand in his evening attire, his breath pluming with each ragged exhalation. The freezing air burned his chest, making his ribs ache. He brought his hand to his forehead, closing his eyes. Was he unwell?

He couldn't explain his behavior. He'd desired her, and that had been all. He'd taken no consideration of Hugo.

Were they engaged already? There had been no announcement. Perhaps, even now, they were addressing the party, their guests raising their glasses to toast the couple. *No, it couldn't be.* Neither Marguerite nor Hugo had mentioned such a thing. His mind was rambling, darting from one thought to the next.

But, he needed to know. Did Hugo intend a proposal? *That kiss!*

His impulse was to return directly, to find Hugo and discover his intentions, but he couldn't face those people again, and he wasn't sure he was ready to hear Hugo's answer. Better to stay outside, letting the night cool his blood.

By the time Mallon re-entered, the madness had leeched away. He felt only weary and chilled. The tree, festooned with ornaments and reaching almost the full height of the atrium, dominated the hall. After his mother's death, his father had stopped bothering much with Christmas, but Mallon remembered how it had been when he was small.

Among the decorations had been a toy soldier. He'd

wanted to keep it, clenching it in his fist. She'd laughed, prising his fingers and explaining that it was for the tree, lifting him to place it upon a branch. Opening a whole box of wooden soldiers on Christmas morning, he'd soon forgotten about it, but he supposed it was here still, hanging somewhere among the other toys and stars and baubles.

Impossible to avoid memories. Everywhere he looked, there was something to remind him of her and his father. It would get easier. He'd been back barely three days, after all.

From beyond closed doors, he could hear the party breaking up—Marguerite's voice, strident, thanking their guests for attending.

Taking refuge in the library, Mallon poured himself a whisky. From the window, he saw the carriages brought around, horses stamping impatiently, tossing their heads in eagerness to get moving. Within minutes, there were footsteps in the hall and the chatter of merry voices.

Tomorrow, he'd talk to Hugo man to man, and find out the seriousness of his intentions. He was no expert on matters of the heart, but it was wrong, surely, for him to deny his nephew's happiness. There had been little enough affection in Mallon's life but there was still time for Hugo.

Mallon knocked back the dregs of his glass. No matter his own feelings, Hugo would come first. It had to be. Whatever attraction Mallon felt for the countess, it must be put aside.

In this, if nothing else, he could do the right thing.

CHAPTER FIFTEEN

GENEVIÈVE TOSSED AGAINST HER PILLOWS. She'd been lying awake for a good hour and without sign of dropping off. It wouldn't do at all. They were riding out with the hunt the next day. More to the point, she'd be sending Lisette with a note for Hugo, inviting him to meet her by the stones on the hill, at Fox Tor.

Rather apt, she thought wryly. The others would be setting off in pursuit of their little fox, while her hunting would be far more efficient. Hugo would come to her. She'd done enough chasing. Time to bring events to the desired conclusion.

If she had anything to do with the matter, Lord Slagsby would not be visiting them once she'd taken Hugo back to France. Annoying that he'd be staying at the hall another week. She had a feeling he'd be just as obnoxious sober as drunk. Even Hugo's announcement of their engagement mightn't stop him from pawing her and making lewd comments. Not that she hadn't had plenty of experience in fending off advances from

Maxim's so-called friends, but it had been a relief to have Mallon step in. Hugo was gallant in his way but, she feared, ineffectual.

Leading Hugo to the mistletoe had certainly done the trick. With a public kiss secured, he'd surely be in the bag tomorrow. The stolen meeting at Fox Tor would provide the perfect romantic setting. He need only begin in the right vein. She'd carry the dowager countess's ring in her pocket, presenting it as part of his inheritance. One mention of her having always admired it and he'd be sure to pop it on her finger.

It was what she'd come for, wasn't it? Making the journey to this godforsaken place. Except that, perhaps, it wasn't as forsaken as it seemed. Rather beautiful, in fact, and its people friendlier than she'd expected. Even with its ghoulish tales of demonic hounds and hairy hands, there was something about the moor that appealed to her. She liked its wild, open spaces and its wide skies.

The dinner itself had been a success. Marguerite had made her approval clear, voicing a desire to return to her family's estate and dropping hints that Hugo would do well to take a French-born wife. Meanwhile, Lord Wulverton had been looking at her from the other end of the table, his expression once again aloof. He still hadn't recognized her, of that she was sure, but nor had he given much impression of being glad of her company.

During their day together, she'd seen another side to him. There had been moments of connection. What did he think of her now? She'd admitted her desire to find a husband, and he could hardly have failed to notice her conduct with Hugo. Lord Wulverton hadn't seemed to judge her—had accepted her as she was, but would he attempt to foil her now that he saw the direction of her hopes?

Was that why he'd intervened as Hugo had led her to dance the second time? Lord Wulverton's gaze had been so intense, she'd worried he would challenge her. His hold upon her waist had been far firmer than was necessary. She'd had the strongest sense he wished to say something. He'd moved with utter surety and with grace but with passion, too, his thigh intruding almost between hers as he'd guided her, his eyes fixed on Geneviève's, excluding all else.

The music had seemed to fade, coming from far away, and she'd been consumed by remembrance, his hands, firm and insistent, pulling her body to meet his. During the waltz, she'd felt herself surrendering as she had in that darkened carriage.

Had he felt it, too? That overwhelming attraction?

Dear God! Had he remembered? Allowing him to hold her so near, had she given herself away? Some mannerism, perhaps, had exposed her.

If so, then it was all the more imperative that she act swiftly. For an instant, she wondered whether to push aside the viscount's domination of her sensual thoughts and seek out Hugo's chamber. Were she to climb into his bed, would he accept the seduction? From chivalry, he'd be inclined to propose as soon as he'd had his release, but she feared it was too clumsy. He was just as likely to recoil in horror.

She needed to think. Better to wait until tomorrow. Daylight tended to add perspective. When Lord Wulverton had made his excuses, exiting abruptly, she'd thought him merely overcome by the warmth of the room. Asking Withers, he'd told her that his master had gone to seek the night air.

Geneviève lay back on the pillow, willing herself to sleep, but it was no use. Doubt was leading her astray. Nothing for it but to go downstairs and heat some milk. At the very least, she'd be glad to get back to her bed after navigating the draughty corridors.

Reaching for her dressing gown, she lit the lamp at her bedside and slipped out, padding down the passage, stepping close to the wall to avoid the squeak of floorboards. She descended the first flight of stairs and paused on the landing. The window there was deep, with a broad seat stretching its width. Outside, the moon shone bright, sending its illumination clear through the glass, lighting the oak-panelled walls.

The moorland was bathed silver. How long ago it seemed since she and Lord Wulverton had set out in the cart. To the west, on the rise of the hill, was the chapel. Strange to think of all those de Wolfe ancestors, who had once stood where she did now, buried in the cold earth of that hill.

The grandfather clock in the hall struck a single, sonorous chime. One in the morning.

As she made to turn away, something caught her attention—a dark shape near the wall of the graveyard. A pony, perhaps, or a black-woolled sheep. The figure rose from its crouch, emerging from the shadows. No animal but a man, moving purposefully down the slope toward the house. She rubbed at her eyes but there was no mistake. It was a man, his head bent forward and shoulders hunched. Who was out at this time?

He'd almost reached the driveway when he looked up and Geneviève caught sight of his face. *Withers?* She gasped and pressed closer to the glass. Her eyes were deceiving her, surely. A man of his age ought to be in bed. The winter cold would be the death of him!

Geneviève strained to follow his path but he disappeared out of sight, around the side of the house. Just then, there was a creak from the upper passageway, a door opening and a shuffling sound, a man's voice, low and cursing.

There was no time to run down the stairs. Instead, she doused her lamp and shrunk back into the corner, concealing herself within the curtains as far as she could.

"Damn him and the whole filthy lot." The voice was familiar, slurred and growing louder. She heard him slip on the stairs, bumping down until he fell upon the landing. More cursing ensued.

Geneviève held her breath, pressing to the wall. She had only to wait for him to pass by and she'd be safe. Thoughts of hot milk were forgotten. A retreat to her bed was all she wished.

"Hell!" Lord Slagsby staggered forward, grasping at the curtains.

To Geneviève's horror, they were suddenly face to face.

"What's this?" Slagsby scowled, drawing her into focus. "Oh, it's you, is it?" He swayed forward, wincing slightly, mumbling to himself. "Hiding in the curtains. Bloody strange thing to do…house full of curs and imbeciles."

Geneviève attempted to duck past but his hand shot out, grasping her above the elbow.

"Not so fast." He looked her over and gave a lazy smile. "I'm on my way to sample more of the viscount's whisky, or his father's I should say. He's not been in this house long enough to call anything his own. Join me, why don't you. You look like you need a drink to loosen you up."

Geneviève reminded herself to stay calm. It shouldn't be difficult to escape him. He was limping a little on his ankle.

"You forget yourself, Lord Slagsby. We're both guests in this house. I, at least, know how to behave." She twisted her head as he stepped closer, his mouth curled in a sneer.

"You weren't always so fine, Countess. Little more than a servant, in fact, doing an old woman's bidding." He gave a derisive snort. "And that husband of yours! Known in every gambling den and brothel from Monte Carlo to Paris."

"Let me pass." Geneviève attempted to keep her voice even. It wouldn't appear well to wake the household and have them witness this little scene.

Slagsby leaned his body into hers. "What did you do, eh, to entice him to marry you? I've heard some stories…" He smirked. "You're no lady, are you? No matter how fine your dresses. You'll give me a kiss, I warrant, and more besides…"

As he lunged, Geneviève tried to bring her knee up but he was too close, pinning her to the wall.

"Get off me, you brute!" Geneviève tried to squirm away.

"On your way to meet someone, I expect. Upstairs, I would have guessed but perhaps you're slumming it, and making do with Down. Meeting you in the scullery, are they? The second footman? More your level, I should think. So here you are—creeping about the house with no fine dress at all. You must be cold, wearing nothing but this."

Without warning, his hand was suddenly under the wrap of her dressing gown, fumbling between her legs, pressing hard enough to make her gasp. "Well, fancy that. Not cold at all. Burning hot!" His fingers delved to enter her through the flimsy fabric of her nightgown.

"Get off me!" cried Geneviève, paying no heed to the loudness of her voice.

Having pulled the sash, her dressing gown fell open easily. In a trice, he'd dragged her nightdress from her shoulder. Despite his inebriation, he was strong, and the force of his assault took her by surprise. He was licking her, leaving a trail of saliva across her collarbone, moving toward her breast.

"Stop it! No!"

He was snuffling wetly across her nipple, then sucking so hard that she gasped in pain.

"Damn you!" She wanted to shout but her tears were

prickling. She tried again to push him away but he was unyielding.

When he drew back it was to grope at the fastening on his trousers, his breath coming heavier, his words more slurred than ever. He brought his face close, his mouth almost slack.

He squeezed her buttock roughly. "Open those legs, and I'll show you a real man."

Gathering all her strength, Geneviève saw her chance. If she leaned forward, she could reach his ear. Fighting her revulsion, she bit down as hard as she could.

Lord Slagsby let out a howl and jerked away. "You little bitch! You'll pay for that."

CHAPTER SIXTEEN

MALLON WOKE to raised voices and a neck stiff from having rested at an unnatural angle in the chair. Who was disturbing the peace at this hour? Not a fracas between the servants, surely. They moved through the house without making a sound; to cause such a commotion in the dead of night would be unthinkable.

Wrenching open the library door, he stepped out into the hall. He'd had just about enough this evening. The noise was coming from the half-landing by the sound of it. *Hell's teeth!* What was going on?

One glance upward showed him the countess cowering, and Lord Slagsby towering over her with his fist raised. A red mist descended at the sight of Geneviève recoiling from her attacker.

"Get your hands off her, you bastard."

Slagsby swayed, looking down, attempting to focus. Recognizing Mallon, his face took on an ugly sneer. "You, was it? Waiting for this foreign slut?"

In a flash, Mallon was up the stairs, his knuckles connecting with Slagsby's nose, followed by a swift punch to the stomach. The younger man crumpled to the floor.

Mallon was hauling Slagsby up by his collar when Hugo appeared on the upper landing, rubbing his eyes. "What's happening? Is it a burglar?"

"Get down here, Hugo."

Seeing Slagsby wiping his bloodied nose on his sleeve, Hugo was all concern. "Whatever's the matter? Did you fall down the stairs, old chap?"

Slagsby shot Mallon a murderous look.

Hugo suddenly noticed the fourth among them. "Good grief! Geneviève! I mean, Countess! Are you all right?"

She was crouching in the corner, attempting to hide her dishevelled appearance. "I'm fine," she said, her voice very small.

Briefly, she threw a glance to Mallon. There was no need for her to speak. He could guess what she wished from him.

"I'll see her safely to her room, and I suggest you accompany your guest back to his. We'll talk about this in the morning."

Seeing his nephew take Slagsby gently around the shoulders, Mallon was struck by how loyal Hugo was. Generous-hearted in the extreme. Edward would have been proud.

"And lock the door on him—for his own safety," Mallon added grimly.

He turned to Geneviève. She was in shock, white-faced and shivering. He fought an impulse to drag Slagsby back and throw him down the stairs.

"You need a stiff drink. Can you walk?"

With a nod, she turned towards him but then looked puzzled, pulling her torn nightdress to make herself decent. With trembling fingers, she attempted to retie the sash of her dressing gown.

By the time she looked up again, Mallon felt he'd turned to stone.

She'd covered herself, but not before he'd seen her breast. Years of visiting the brothels of Constantinople had made him familiar with the female form. He knew it in all its variety and there had been only one woman who'd borne this particular mark.

It had been too dark to see her face—a fact that had added to the frisson of the encounter. How many women had such a mole? A coincidence, surely? But, as he looked into her eyes, he knew that she stood before him.

Her expression was shifting—a flush entering her cheeks, her eyes growing wider. *She knew!* Whatever she saw, now, in his face—this shock of recognition—she'd been waiting for it.

He was taken again to that night on the train. Her breast heavy in his palm. His thumb circling the dark areola, bringing it to an enticing peak. Tracing the satin smoothness of her skin, he'd found the raised beauty spot to the left of her nipple, tonguing it before taking her breast deep into his mouth. His loins flared at that remembrance, and at what had come afterward.

Hadn't she been straddling him at the time? Teasing him from their earlier coupling? He remembered her sigh as she lowered herself onto him. His groans of satisfaction had driven her on, taking him deep, then tantalizing him with slow withdrawal, only to plunge again, crying out as he filled her. His moans he'd stifled against her breast, suckling the fullness, revelling in the softness of its curve against his chin and cheek—and that mole!

He was not mistaken!

LORD WULVERTON HAD GIVEN her a large brandy and found a blanket from somewhere. He seemed reluctant to meet her eyes, poking instead at the fire he'd relit. From the hallway, the clock chimed two. Had only an hour passed?

Events had happened in a blur. Geneviève recalled Slagsby shaking her, his fingers pressing bruising hard. She'd fought back, kicking his ankle, then catching him partially in the groin with her fist, but not enough to disable him. He'd had the face of a madman as he'd raised his arm to strike her. She'd been waiting for the blow when the viscount had shouted. He'd bounded up, taking the steps three at a time, falling upon Slagsby like a demon.

The relief had been overwhelming. With the fight drained from her body, her knees hadn't wanted to hold her anymore, so she'd curled up by the curtains.

She hadn't wanted to look at Hugo, nor Lord

Wulverton. It was shaming, to have been called those names. Slagsby was a beast. Men didn't even treat whores like that. Or perhaps they did. What did she know? Perhaps she'd been lucky with Maxim. He'd never hit her, at least.

However, there had been times when she'd thought herself little better than the women selling themselves at the docks in Marseille, despite the ring on her finger.

Lord Slagsby was loathsome but there was some truth in what he'd said. Her contract involved a marriage license but it amounted to almost the same thing. Ownership of her body in return for security.

No wonder Maxim's circle had gossiped about her— the little convent stray taken into the bosom of a noble family, climbing her way into the bed of the count himself, and extracting no less than a wedding ring. If Slagsby had heard rumors about her, then who else? Not Hugo—at least not yet. She'd have to talk to him, as soon as possible, giving him her version of events. Better that than for him to hear Slagsby's putrid gossip.

She'd felt such a rush of gratitude when the viscount had stepped in, saving her from Slagsby's attack, but she had another problem to deal with now.

Lord Wulverton's face had shown her everything.

It had never occurred to her that he'd remember such a thing as the mole on her breast. Didn't other women have such marks? How could he know it was her?

That night on the train had been madness. A stupid and imprudent whim. But how liberating! And how satisfying—being caressed by a man truly of her choosing, taking what *she* desired.

Her attraction to the viscount had been threatening her resolve to marry Hugo, for she found Lord Wulverton more purposeful, more impassioned, and more stirring in every way. But, it was Hugo who'd inherited Château Rosseline, where she'd found a true home.

It was there she belonged, not upon the moors, however beautiful she thought them. If she could but return to the château, and with a respectable husband at her side, mightn't she conquer those who'd once scorned her. Her charm and intelligence would help her gain her heart's desire. Marrying Hugo would be the first step in achieving that.

She raised the brandy to her lips, savoring its bitter sweetness. Whatever happened next, she had money. Society might ostracize her but she'd never be destitute.

When Lord Wulverton turned, his face was without expression. He remained standing, examining her for several moments before speaking.

"There's no need for us to discuss why you were in your nightgown on the stairs. I don't need to hear whatever story you'll spin for me."

Her pique flared but Geneviève said nothing. If he wished to believe badly of her, it would be almost impossible to correct him.

"I'll cut to the chase. You're here at the invitation of my sister-in-law, who appears satisfied to allow you to court the attention of my nephew." His eyes narrowed.

"Hugo may be a man in years but he's an innocent. Meanwhile, you, Madam, are an adventuress!"

Gazing into her glass, Geneviève willed herself to remain poised. She would have her say. That, at least, she was entitled to. "It's true that I desire respectability and an elevated position in Society. I have wealth, but my modest beginnings are against me. There are circles in which I'm unwelcome and those who are swift to malign my character." Looking up, she met Lord Wulverton's glare, fixing him with her own. "That, dear sir, is something I intend to remedy."

"You think respectability can be acquired by taking a husband of good breeding?" He stood tall above her. "No woman who behaves as you do will ever be truly respectable. Don't deny your true nature, for I know you and I call you out! You're a harlot, flaunting your carnality for the entrapment of men!"

For a moment, Geneviève thought she might laugh. Lord Wulverton had called Hugo naïve! As for 'respectable' women, she suspected she was not alone in her employment of wiles. Even the most well-bred ladies must occasionally make use of what God had given them.

She might have voiced that thought aloud, or any number of similar notions. Instead, she found herself saying, "You know nothing of me, my lord."

His reply was immediate. "You will own, surely, that I know something, or are you forgetting what occurred on the train from Marseille?"

Geneviève felt her annoyance flare. "If you wish to

take the moral high ground, I recall no proposal of marriage before you took what you wanted."

"My recollection is that the lady was far from unwilling. I didn't take anything that wasn't freely offered."

Geneviève gritted her teeth. "Our pleasure in one another was equal. If you insist otherwise, I must call you a hypocrite."

The viscount waved his hand in dismissal. "A man's actions are not scrutinized in the same way—are not judged as those of women. Our reputation is not so fragile."

"Indeed! A man is applauded for his conquests, a woman reviled. Eve, the seductress sinner, and Adam, the guiltless lamb, led astray. Isn't this your boorish opinion?"

"You attempt to wriggle away with clever words, but I will have an answer. What are your intentions toward Hugo?"

Geneviève folded back the blanket from her knees before rising. Walking over to the decanters, she took her time in selecting and pouring more into her glass. "He's a charming young man."

"One with wealth and a title, whom you intend to deceive into his marriage vows, making him believe you love him when you mean only to use his position for your own betterment."

Geneviève did allow herself to laugh at that. "Where a man believes himself in love, a woman need provide only a little encouragement."

"Love!" He spat the word. "Love serves only to blind us to the nature of the other."

He spoke so vehemently, Geneviève was brought up sharply. "You don't believe in love?"

"I do not."

"Then, what do you believe...where women are concerned?"

A muscle was twitching in his jaw and his eyes had grown almost black. The bitterness in his tone was unmistakable. "You profess love but only as it suits you. You are constant only where it provides material benefit. You manipulated me, Madam, but I am no longer deceived, and I will not allow you to play with the heart of one who is gullible. You may feign gentility and the sincerity of love, but I know your true nature. Ruled by your passions, with no thought of virtue, or constancy, you're not to be trusted!"

Ice had been stealing through her at the tone of his voice, but then the ice turned to fire, and her indignation began to grow hot. If the viscount wished to preach, she'd happily show him his own 'true nature'.

Geneviève pulled the sash of her dressing gown. As he reached the end of his tirade, she looked him directly in the eyes, letting the two halves of the garment part. As if absentmindedly, she brushed her fingers across the front of her flimsy nightdress.

"You think me a whore because I have a mind of my own and refuse to act the virgin; because I desire physical pleasure in the same way as a man."

He faltered into remarkable stillness. Where his voice had risen, gathering in outrage, her own was measured. She moved the torn fabric to one side, exposing the curve of pale skin. "This is how you expect me to behave, is it not?" Already, the imprint of her assailant's fingers was visible where he'd squeezed her breast violently. A welt was rising where Lord Slagsby had raked his teeth.

"You saw this?" Geneviève touched the mole. "A pretty thing, Maxim always thought it. And you, Lord Wulverton? I recall you kissing more than my hand, not so long ago."

"You mean to provoke me." His voice was tight.

Geneviève continued to speak softly as she came forward. When she stood before him, close enough that he might reach out and touch her, he licked his lips, his eyes dropping to where she teased her nipple, drawing it to a point between her fingers.

He made no move to step back, his eyes solely upon her body.

"You censure me, yet you wish nothing more than to ravish me again," she murmured. "We're alone, so you may do as you wish. I shan't protest."

She paused before speaking again, raising the volume of her voice, her manner more assertive. "Here, before the fire? Or would you rather bend me over where we stand?" Bringing her hand to his groin, she found what she knew would be there, the hardness of his desire.

She uttered the last with a cry of defiance. "Remember to leave payment as you did before!"

A dark shadow crossed Lord Wulverton's face, as if he couldn't decide whether to strike her or take her at her word. However, he stepped back, his lip curling in disdain.

"I concede that I cannot control every base impulse of my masculinity. However, tonight, I choose to temper those passions rather than being their slave."

She was irked to realize that he'd claimed the last word.

CHAPTER SEVENTEEN

Withers drawing back the curtains allowed the mid-morning sun to enter. "Pardon me, m'lord. I thought it best to wake you."

Mallon's head was pounding. He couldn't remember how much he'd drunk but, as he shielded his eyes from the sudden flood of daylight, other events from the past evening pulled into focus.

Retiring to his bed, his blood had been fevered. Geneviève had made a fool of him, or he'd made one of himself. Either way, it was a damnable situation.

They'd each spoken their mind, and there would be no more lies. He knew exactly what sort of woman he was dealing with, and she was no better than his mother. Too bold with her sensuality, too inclined to act on impulse, too adept at concealment. Like his mother, she was a breaker of hearts—and Mallon had no intention of placing his own on a salver, as his father had done, to be sliced into pieces.

He could never forget those years of his father's

embittered, cold detachment. Mallon's childhood had been a cruel lesson in betrayal—not just on his mother's part, but his father's, too. They had both let him down.

The thought of becoming like his father both repulsed and terrified Mallon. He'd never inflict that on any child of his own. Better to remain a bachelor and avoid such tangled pain.

Mallon had spent most of the night counting the chimes as the hours passed, all the while debating how he could permit the countess's continued presence.

It would be awkward in the extreme. As for Hugo, the poor fool might think himself besotted but he had little idea about women—and none at all about Geneviève, who would never be content with an innocent like Hugo. Mallon imagined she'd have a string of lovers before the first year of marriage was out.

"I've brought a tray, m'lord, seeing as the main breakfast has been cleared."

With a sigh, Mallon poured from the coffee pot. The kipper he pushed aside.

"Thank you, Withers. I've meant to ask how things are on the estate. I must meet with Scroggins, to find out about the cattle."

"Aye, m'lord. He'll be glad to talk to ye. He's gathered 'em safely in the shippon, what with the snow coming. Take a care going in, as we've the ram tethered by the door and he's in a foul mood at losing his liberty. We've plenty of hay stored in the loft above, an' Scroggins has put up the rowan sprigs to keep the beasties safe."

"Ah yes! Excellent!" It had been some time since Mallon had heard mention of that custom—rowan to keep away the roaming imps and witches of the winter moor. Nonsense, of course, but it was not for him to interfere.

"And how are you, Withers? Keeping well?"

The butler had been around since his grandfather's day. At some point, Mallon supposed, he'd have to broach the subject of a well-earned retirement. He'd be welcome to stay in the house, of course. Mallon had no intention of turning anyone out. Wulverton Hall had been Withers's home for a lifetime; it was unlikely that he had alternative plans.

Withers, Mallon noted, had failed to reply. Instead, he was staring vacantly out of the window and was looking every one of his eighty years. Was it more? Mallon could hardly begin to say.

"Lost in your thoughts, Withers? Hope you're not out of sorts."

"Sorry, m'lord. Just looking at the ravens. They gathered about the hall before the passing of your father, and Lord Edward. They'ums are still about."

Mallon took another gulp of coffee. He knew what Withers was getting at. The raven was an ill omen, a harbinger of death. If he didn't get some Seltzers inside him soon, it might be his death the ravens were cawing for.

"If that's all m'lord." Withers shuffled back toward the door. "I've left some hot water in the pitcher."

"Thank you. Nothing for now." Mallon stirred himself to sit up, holding his head gingerly.

Except there was something else. Mallon needed to ask Withers about his brother. He hadn't known the escaped convict was Silas until one of the farmers had mentioned it yesterday. With everything that had happened, he'd not had a chance to take Withers aside. No wonder the poor man was talking of ravens and gazing onto the moor. He must be worried sick, imagining his brother out there alone.

It was his duty, as viscount, to look out for those in his care, the tenants on his land and the servants in this house. Hangover or not, certain things had to be dealt with.

However, for now, he needed to catch Hugo, and he'd better get a move on. What time was the hunt setting off? Eleven?

"MORE MUDDY FOOTPRINTS!" declared Marguerite, looking at the hearthrug in Hugo's room. "With guests in the house, it's really too much!"

Mallon stood in the doorway, watching his sister-in-law scuff her slipper against the marks. Despite the success of her entertainments, she didn't appear in a very festive mood. It was hard, he supposed, coping with everything on her own. She had, after all, been running the house single-handedly since Edward's demise, and that of his father.

She began plumping the cushions on Hugo's sofa. "I've been letting the dogs prowl about, with this dreadful convict on the loose, but they'll have to stay in the kitchen if they're going to bring this filth with them."

Marguerite didn't know, then, that it was Silas who'd escaped. Before her time, of course. It pained Mallon. To her, he was just another ne'er-do-well.

Muttering about table settings and making sure luncheon would be served promptly, she swept out.

She'd been talking about her late brother's vineyard the other night. It might do her good to have a bit of sunshine. Now Mallon was back, there was nothing to stop her from going. He'd encourage her to make the trip, once all the hubbub of Christmas was dealt with.

Mallon sighed. His plans to speak to Hugo would have to wait. The young swain had set off already, along with the others taking part in the hunt.

As he made to leave, pulling the door closed behind him, something caught on Mallon's brogue. The carpet was fraying and he'd stepped into a stray loop. Like rather many things at Wulverton, it was in need of attention, the rod having come loose, leaving the threads to unravel. He stooped to free himself, and it was then the piece of paper caught his eye. A laundry list, or some such, dropped by one of the maids, which had found its way under the carpet's edge.

Since his soldiering days, he'd not been able to abide disorder. The hearth embers were sufficient to burn a scrap of paper; he could simply toss it in. However, it wasn't just a piece of paper but an envelope—and bearing Hugo's name, in an extravagant hand.

It was still sealed.

Mallon fought with his conscience only briefly. Tearing it open, he read:

My darling,
I must see you. Find a way to leave the hunt and come to me.
I'll be waiting at Fox Tor.
Yours, with love and anticipation,
G.

She certainly hadn't wasted any time. Mallon crushed the note angrily in his fist. When had she pushed it beneath Hugo's door? Early that morning? Mere hours after offering herself to him.

He'd thought she might abandon her aspirations regarding Hugo, considering last night's events. Clearly, Mallon had underestimated her. Were Hugo to deliver a proposal, it would be much harder to persuade him to break it off. The boy was honorable and would be loath to break a promise—whatever the circumstances.

Fortunately, it appeared that Mallon still had time to intercede. Hugo had never seen the note. The countess would be waiting at the tor in vain.

Mallon threw the papers into the fire, where they curled and flared.

GENEVIÈVE HAD learnt to ride at Maxim's insistence. She'd soon become proficient, and the resulting freedom had been a revelation. Her happiest hours had since been spent on horseback.

From the bottom of the hill, the tor stones were barely discernible against the slated clouds. The palette was sombre in comparison to the azure heavens she'd left behind, and the vibrant yellows and pinks of the flowers growing around Château Rosseline. Nevertheless, the landscape invigorated her. Its beauty was undeniable.

Reaching the summit, she tethered her pony beside lichened boulders engulfed in the smell of earth and age. There were no trees this high on the moor—barely a bush, even. She'd felt exposed, at first, but a low mist was closing in, filling the air with dampness, still and quiet—the cold breath of the moor on her cheek.

How long had she been waiting? Hugo had set off with a cheery wave, calling that he'd see her soon. Purposefully, she'd held back, to make it easier to peel away from the other riders. Was that the far-off cry of the hounds she could hear, and the horn of the master huntsman? From further down the hill, she thought she discerned a shout, or was it merely the caw of a passing crow? The mist, curling and rolling, seemed to deaden sound. Meanwhile, her own breathing appeared much louder than usual.

Geneviève shivered. She was quite distant from the chapel, but she thought of what she'd seen there, just the day before—or what she'd thought she'd seen. Again, she had the feeling of being watched by unseen eyes. She'd been a ninny, conjuring ridiculous terrors. Her imagination had been seized by reading *The Hound of the Baskervilles* and by the legend of the devil's Wisht Hounds. She ought to feel ashamed of herself. A grown woman and so impressionable!

Of course, there were other things to be afraid of besides ghostly hounds and piskies. The convict was out there somewhere, wasn't he? Alive or dead? He might even be hiding nearby, among the rocks. She glanced over her shoulder at the great monoliths behind. Lord Wulverton had spoken of him with tenderness, but this Silas was a stranger to her, and he'd been locked up all this time. Who knew how that affected a man? Even those who went in entirely sane must emerge half-demented after years of deprivation and constraint. She'd rather die than endure it herself.

I might ride back to the hall.

Geneviève could barely see more than a few feet ahead. Heading toward the boulders where she'd tied her mount, they sprouted an arm, shaking it at her, causing her to scream, but it was only the pony, tossing its mane. It gazed at her stolidly, through eyes long-lashed, before returning to its steady grazing.

She placed her hand on its side. He, at least, was real. There was comfort in his soft snorts and his warmth. Strange to feel more afraid of what you couldn't see than what you could, but there was something chilling about the immensity of the moor and its cloaked vastness.

Was that a horse? She swore to hearing hooves. Wasn't Lady Howard's coach pulled by horses—headless ones? What were you supposed to do if you saw them? Closing her eyes tight, she leaned her forehead against the pony's flank. If she didn't look, they'd pass by. Devilish things only consumed those foolish enough to invite their interest.

She pinched herself. Her imagination was running away again. If she could hear a horse, it must be Hugo.

He was riding a white dappled mare and would be invisible until he was right upon her.

"Hugo! I'm here." Her voice sounded thin.

There was no reply but the hooves were growing louder, beating rhythmically across the turf. Whatever creature it was, the beast was snorting heavily. With numb fingers she began to untie her mount. Better to take the saddle again. She'd feel safer on horseback, though the pony was skittering, eager to get away.

The approaching force loomed out of the mist, galloping toward her. Not white but black; a huge stallion, its eyes rolling in its head, rearing up so close that her own pony cowered in fear. She'd barely gotten her feet in the stirrups when her mount bolted.

Terrified, there was nothing she could do but hold on tightly and pray. They weren't racing back the way they'd come but to the west, the pony leaping rocks and splashing through small streams crossing the hillside. Still, she could see nothing, the mist being just as thick lower down as it had been at the tor.

From behind, a deep voice called to her to stop. As if she'd do that when some demon had been conjured to pursue her!

The ground had levelled out and the pony was slowing to a canter, its panting ragged. Still, she could hear the hooves of the demon rider.

"Keep going!" she urged, giving the hardest kicks she could muster. The pony whinnied in protest, but took to the gallop again, carrying them swiftly across the moor. Too late, she saw the sheep—perhaps ten of them, standing close together, their pale wool disguising them in the mist.

Jerking the reins, she pulled the pony's head round. It seemed to twist in mid-air and the world began to spin. Even as Geneviève felt herself flying, she heard the voice commanding to go no further. Then, the mist rose up to consume her.

CHAPTER EIGHTEEN

TENDRILS OF HAIR clung damply across Geneviève's forehead. Mud slurped at her boots and her hem was muck-encrusted. Dirt caked the ankle of her stockings. In short, she was sodden and miserable. Her mount had disappeared into the mist and a fine veil of drizzle was falling,

She'd rolled as she landed and, fortunately, onto moss. Assessing herself, Geneviève found no injury beyond some tenderness to her right elbow. There would doubtless be bruises but she'd only feel them properly the next day.

Her pride, however, had taken rather a beating. As Lord Wulverton stood over her, she realized all too well what a mooncalf she'd been. A demon galloping after her indeed!

Hurrying to her side, his face was ashen. Anxious that she'd broken her neck, she supposed. He'd have had the devil's own job explaining that to Hugo!

"I take it you plan to help me up," she grumbled. "I've no wish to catch pneumonia."

Seeing she appeared unhurt, his face grew still, his expression indecipherable. He made no apology for having frightened her, nor did he berate her for racing off through the mist. If he was angry, he concealed it well. Geneviève waited for a tirade in the manner of the previous night, but he seemed disinclined to argue with her.

"We're on the edge of the mire, and this mist makes it too dangerous to venture back." He looked about him, as if searching for some landmark. "I'd guess we're no more than a mile from The Saracen's Head, so it makes sense to go there."

She might have been made of feathers and silk as he swung her up, lifting her effortlessly. It occurred to her that she ought to feel angry with him—for interfering, besides anything else—but she supposed she could hardly blame him.

It was indeed pleasant to be in his arms. Hers, she wrapped close about his neck, with only a small thrill of gratification at seeing the mud she transferred to his collar. She leaned into him as he carried her, resting her head on his shoulder. His heartbeat seemed far steadier than hers.

Once mounted, with Mallon behind her in the saddle, she felt the weight of his coat placed about her shoulders, warm from his body and carrying a masculine scent.

Despite the mist, the horse seemed to know where to step, its eyes attuned to the subtle shades of green indicating safety or danger. Only once did it stumble; then, she felt Wulverton tighten his arm around her waist, pulling her closer to him.

It was as if the world had disappeared and only they existed, plodding through the dense bank of mist, his chest solid behind her. Even with his proximity, her damp clothing invited the chill, drawing cold into her bones. The sun was already dipping from the sky and the temperature dropping.

At last, a familiar smell carried to her nose, peat smoke and the scent of cooking meat. The next moment, the steeply-angled roof of the inn emerged fog-wreathed. Light was shining from its mullioned windows, dull illumination through the crawling mist, but a welcome haven.

HER HANDS WERE FROZEN white and her teeth chattering as they entered the old coaching inn. Geneviève had never felt more bedraggled. The ringlets that had hung prettily over her shoulder now straggled wetly.

With a room secured for each of them, she made haste to hers. It was a sorry sight that met her in the mirror. Forlornly, she attempted to re-pin her hair and scrape the muck from her boots. However, within a few minutes, there was a soft knock upon the door. Opening it, Geneviève found a young woman had been sent to her.

"Beg pardon, Miss, but the gentleman asked if we'd summat fer ye to change into." She bobbed a curtsey and extended her arm to offer a length of green wool serge. "'Twas one of the late mistress's, wot she never wore, on account o' fallin' ill afore she'd the chance."

Geneviève was in no position to refuse, though the dress had clearly been hanging for some time and was not in the latest fashion, or any style she was aware of from the past decade. Still, it was clean and would make her a sight more presentable.

It was with some trepidation that she returned downstairs. The inn was busy. She glanced into the bar as she went past and it was already nearly full. No women, she noted. Tucked away at home with the children and the laundry, and stew to make, while the menfolk shared a pipe and huddled together exchanging their gossip.

Lord Wulverton had commandeered the snug, sitting by a fire heaped high and blazing. He reclined in his usual manner, legs stretched toward the hearth, as relaxed as if The Saracen's Head were his sitting room.

Geneviève feared what he might wish to say to her. She wasn't in the mood for an argument, and he hadn't ridden out to Fox Tor merely to wish her a good day. Somehow, he'd discovered her intended rendezvous. Had he spoken with Hugo? Was the game up? Suddenly, she felt weary of it all.

Bugger the lot of them! What she really wanted was something to eat. She'd taken only a light breakfast and it was well into the afternoon. Kitchen smells had permeated even to her bedchamber, making her mouth water as she'd fastened the last of the buttons on her borrowed dress.

"At last!" Wulverton commented as she approached. "There's steak pie on the way. If you'd been much longer, I'd have been tempted to eat both portions."

She seated herself opposite, accepting the hot toddy he'd ordered for her. It smelt of cloves and cinnamon and warming ginger. Whatever game he was playing, she appreciated the creature comforts that went with it. Trying to butter her up, she supposed—putting her at ease before ambushing her with an ultimatum. There were only a few days until Christmas. He wouldn't ask her to leave, surely—not so close to the actual celebrations. It was a miserable thought. Despite having to endure the likes of Mrs. Wapshot, Geneviève had grown rather fond of Wulverton Hall.

When their plates arrived, piled high and steaming with gravy, Lord Wulverton tucked in with gusto, and Geneviève didn't need any convincing to do the same.

Despite the awkwardness of their situation, she found herself relaxing in his company. Sitting by the hearth, enjoying their plain yet satisfying meal, she was almost able to forget the thorny circumstances that had led them here. Able to forget, almost, what her plans had been that morning. How straightforward it might have been if they had met in the proper way, or had never met until this moment—finding themselves both seated before the fire, drawing comfort from the inn's simple welcome.

She dashed away that thought. It was fanciful to imagine otherwise.

Nevertheless, she heard herself telling him of the cassoulet she remembered the nuns making, richly flavored with garlic and cloves, the haricot beans soft and buttery, and the duck melting as it touched her tongue.

Her upkeep at the convent had come with a price, obliging her to help most days in the preparation of meals. If she hadn't gone to the dowager Comtesse Rosseline as a companion she might, at a pinch, have found employment in the château kitchen.

"It sounds a darned sight more appetizing than the grub we were given at school," said Mallon, consuming the last of his pie crust. "But, don't tell Mrs. Fuddleby about your secret culinary skills, unless you want to be given an apron. She's already taken a shine to you, I'd say."

Geneviève returned his smile. "I expect Marguerite has taught her some French recipes, but it would be a pleasure. The kitchens are the heart of the house, are they not?"

Mallon looked at her most curiously, almost as if seeing her for the first time. "I used to find that true, when I was a boy. It was only years later that I thought to wonder at the cook always having a cake to make when I appeared at the kitchen door. Whatever had been troubling me seemed less acute by the time I'd finished beating the mixture."

"You had the sweet tooth, like all children." Geneviève eyed him playfully. Noting he seemed interested in the steak pie yet remaining on her plate, she pushed it toward him. "And what was your favorite of the cakes? The famous British scones, perhaps, or your Victoria Sponge?"

Mallon inclined his head in thanks and applied his fork to a large chunk of beef. "Both excellent choices but not my favorites." He chewed thoughtfully. "It's a tough call, but I'd say Bread and Butter Pudding."

"Is this what they serve at Buckingham Palace, when they wish to impress visitors from the other royal houses of Europe?" Geneviève raised an eyebrow. "A pudding made of bread?"

Mallon chuckled. "It's much nicer than it sounds, although it works perfectly well with stale bread."

Geneviève wrinkled her nose.

"Mrs. Fuddleby puts plenty of cream in the custard and a generous handful of sultanas. You can make a wish as you sprinkle them in. At least, that's what she told me. I'll ask her to make one for us, and you'll see."

Geneviève felt her heart beat a little faster. Did he wish her to stay? "I understand. Such recipes are made with love. When the woman who cares for you makes this dish, it cannot be anything other than delicious."

Mallon dabbed his mouth with his napkin, looking suddenly a little embarrassed.

Although the meal had been generous, latticed apple tart followed, after which they both settled back, replete. The warmth of the room and her satisfied belly were making Geneviève feel unexpectedly content. More drinks were brought, and they sat in affable silence, listening to the crackle of the flames.

Yet, Geneviève couldn't set aside all unease. Now they'd eaten, he meant, surely, to address the circumstances under which he'd sought her out. She needed a diversion—an alternative subject of conversation. The weather always provided safe ground.

With forced cheerfulness, she remarked, "Everyone keeps saying snow's coming but I'm not convinced. Will we see a white Christmas, do you think, or only more of this dreadful fog?"

It was a clumsy attempt.

He surveyed her through half-closed lids but when he gave his reply, it was with disarming sincerity. "Each season has its own beauty. You should see the summer. When I was a boy, I'd wander, sunburnt as a nut, my sleeves and trousers dyed with blackberry stains and hands clammy with sweet juices."

He held up his glass of spiced cider to the firelight, admiring its rich color before taking another draught. "There's much that's bewitching but the moor can also be a melancholy place. Even in the warmest months, you'll find snow in its shaded hollows. For the swaling, they burn the heather and furze to clear the way for new growth, before digging in the ash. Then everything awakens, young and alive and made anew, and the gorse flames gold."

'You should be here' he'd said. Geneviève found her heart lifting, not just at the remark, uttered more in politeness than invitation, but because he was talking as he had before, as they'd sat beside one another on the cart, visiting each homestead. His Lordship, for all his maddening ways, conversed with her as an equal, rather than in flattery of her physical charms or in a condescending way, to show off his cleverness.

He asked softly, "Have you felt it? The sky gazing at you?"

The words were like an enchantment, pulling Geneviève closer.

"During my time in the desert, beneath the tent of that other sky, I drew some comfort, thinking of the sun that blazed looking down with subtler warmth upon the moor. The same stars, too—points of light in the heavens, and the moon's illumination above. I'd go to sleep imagining myself beside the lake or under the great shadow of the Dewerstone, with the moorland air fresh on my cheek and the moss cool beneath my back."

She felt a keen desire for him to continue addressing her in this way, crediting her with the same ability to respond to the landscape he loved.

Though aware of the hubbub of chatter from the bar across the hallway, Geneviève felt all else fading away, just as it had when they'd been riding together. There was only Lord Wulverton speaking softly, filling her ear with his confidences, appearing to *need* to tell her as much as she desired to listen.

Although they were alone, she found herself whispering. "Does the moor have so many secrets?"

"You might live here all your life and never comprehend them. Its mysteries are matched only by those we hold within us."

Her heart lurched. The previous evening, he'd made it clear he thought her a social climber of the worst sort, using her body to further herself. He meant, surely, to remind her of the deceits she'd perpetrated, exerting her charm over poor Hugo, who was as helpless in matters of love as an adolescent girl.

Geneviève knew that she ought to retire, before he broached what must surely be on his mind, but she couldn't bear to leave.

He'd lent her the book, of course. She might comment on that. "I can see why Conan Doyle came here, to research the enigmas of the moor, finding inspiration for his novel."

In her recent nights of sleeplessness, she'd burnt her candle to the quick, reading of the Baskerville Hound and its terrible curse. She could see how cleverly the legends of Dartmoor had been drawn upon.

"It makes for compulsive reading…and the ending! So horrible!"

A frown crossed his face. "The dangers of the moor are real."

"Those damnable mires, waiting to suck you under!" She gave a laugh but it emerged brittle, constrained too greatly by her nerves.

Wulverton remained serious. "Grimpen Mire, as described by Conan Doyle in his book, is inspired by the very place you almost rode into. If you hadn't been thrown, your horse would have taken you where I couldn't have followed. There would've been no saving you. It looks like solid grass but it's an illusion. The quagmire moss is no more than a quaking blanket, concealing dark pools of liquid peat. One false step means death."

The last he spoke with great emphasis. His hand shook as he reached for his drink, taking a deep draft.

She'd hardly *chosen* to guide her horse in the direction of the mire. She'd not even known it was there! As for the speed at which her mount had taken her, that was entirely due to the viscount's fearsome arrival.

Geneviève drew herself upright, intending to explain herself, but he interrupted as she began, his expression so stern she was obliged to close her mouth again to prevent her lip from trembling.

"You've heard, perhaps, more of my mother than I've told you?"

The directness of his manner obliged Geneviève to lower her eyes. Mrs. Fuddleby had been gossiping and she'd listened, wanting to know more. Now that she had the chance, she felt rather ashamed of herself.

"Among the graves I visited, beside the chapel, one bears her name, but there is no body. She ventured out to meet her lover—the man my father had employed to help him oversee the estate. They'd arranged to meet here, as it happens, with plans to elope. Having waited for several hours, he went looking for her. Like tonight, there was a mist, and she must have lost her way. Neither she nor her horse were ever found."

"Surely not…" Geneviève experienced a shiver of horror, realizing what he was telling her. She had assumed the late viscountess to have died of natural causes.

He paused, looking grim.

"Her just dessert, some might say, for abandoning her children, as well as her husband." His face was hard. "My father never forgave us for being hers, nor did he remarry. The only affection Edward and I received was from our nursery maid and the other staff. As soon as we were old enough, he sent us away to Eton."

His confession was startling to her. "Monstrous! Whatever the sins of your mother, you were not to blame."

"True, but perhaps my father thought we weren't his at all."

Geneviève bit her lip. What right had she to comment upon the misdeeds of others, or the acts they were driven to through loneliness or betrayal?

Lord Wulverton angled his body away from her. The intimacy she'd glimpsed had vanished.

"It wasn't only we who suffered. There was our stableman, Withers's brother, Silas. You recall I spoke of him? My father had him convicted of stealing, since he was responsible for the yard and every horse in it."

He passed his hand over his face, looking all at once weary.

"My father should never have married her. She was unsuited to the moor, and they were unsuited for each other. Their union was destined to unhappiness."

He looked pointedly at Geneviève. "I've vowed never to find myself in a similar position, and my vow extends to Hugo. I'll do all I can to prevent him from entering into an ill-advised marriage."

He'd come to it at last and there was nothing Geneviève could say to defend herself.

CHAPTER NINETEEN

Mallon shrugged off his jacket, casting it onto the bed. What a bloody mess! He tugged loose his tie. He hadn't wanted to find himself in this position, of being so close to Geneviève alone.

Riding out to Fox Tor, he'd been ready to take her down several pegs—to revoke her invitation and ask her to leave. How could he have known that her horse would bolt, taking her off like that, to the west of the tor?

There lay the most treacherous of all the mires. He'd tried to stop her, but she hadn't heard him calling, or had ignored him, or hadn't been able to pull up her mount.

He'd been assailed by a fear worse than any he harbored over Hugo's future. The mire had a habit of claiming lives. It had taken her hadn't it—his mother, and Geneviève had almost ridden into that same danger.

Some angel had been watching over her, to make her

tumble as she had, throwing her to safety. Seeing her on the ground, mud-splattered but alive, any anger he'd felt had ebbed away. He'd wanted to kneel and pull her to him, to kiss her until she gasped for breath, to hold her tightly and keep her there. Instead, she might have died and been lost to him forever.

The thought sickened him—made his mind swirl black with despair.

He sensed that she understood more about him than he'd first realized. Different as their childhoods had been, they'd both been raised by 'strangers'—she at the convent, and he at Eton. Of course, he'd had more of a family than she. He'd had Edward, at least, and the knowledge of a father still living, even if he'd bestowed little enough affection upon his sons. And they'd both sought out new places to belong—he with his regiment, and she at her beloved château.

She seemed to understand something of the moor, too, its beauty and its majesty. He thought of the things he might show her, sharing what he loved about this wild, untamed land. He'd never before wanted to reveal that part of himself to anyone. Never wanted to allow a woman to get that close—to see what truly mattered to him.

Ridiculous nonsense!

How could one prolong such feelings for a woman? Men were asses to allow their amorous emotions to rule them. Look at what it had done to his father. His broken heart had robbed him of the ability to show love to anyone or to take any joy in living at all. He'd become a bitter old man.

Permitting himself feelings for Geneviève could only lead to disaster. Deceit came too easily for her to be capable of fidelity, showing him one face and another to Hugo.

She feigned gentility when she was as brazen as any courtesan. No matter that he partly admired her for that very audacity. No matter that he understood the need for her to keep that side of her nature hidden. He knew the world's hypocrisy, men being judged in one way for their sexual exploits and women in another. It was simply the way of the world. A woman's virtue hinged on her constancy.

He found her attractive, but more than that. Knowing she was the woman on the train did nothing to diminish his desire. Quite the reverse. Were it not for the complication of Hugo, he'd have acted upon that desire before now.

Whatever he was feeling, whatever the hell this was, it was a passing whim. A temporary state of insanity. How could it be more?

Mallon unfastened his cuffs, then pulled off his shirt. He'd try to forget she was just two doors away—forget what he wanted to do.

He'd requested a bath be filled in the room between their two chambers. He'd heard the water running and seen the maid going out. For now, he should get clean, climb under the covers, and seek blessed release in sleep. The rest he'd think about tomorrow.

OPENING THE DOOR, he saw Geneviève had gotten there before him. He felt a flush of irritation. Was he to have no peace?

Her head was only just visible above the lip of the tub, her hair half-tumbled, pinned haphazardly.

To do anything other than retreat was an invasion of her privacy. After all, he'd expounded on the state of her morals, it would be outrageous for him to abuse the situation, yet he found himself compelled to look upon her. A single curl clung wetly to the nape of her neck, dark against pale skin.

As he watched, she extended a leg—long and slender, hooking it over the bath's rim, then did the same with the other, raising herself slightly. He caught a glimpse of full breasts and rosy nipples.

Her hand was sliding down, stroking beneath the water. He could be in no doubt as to what she was doing. She reached lower, lifting her hips. Almost above the surface of the water. Almost.

Even a saint would have had trouble turning away, and he was no saint.

Beneath the towel at his waist, he grew hard.

Her breath was coming in shivering gulps, until she threw back her head, gasping her release.

Still he stood, unmoving. Before long, she'd realize he was there. There was still time for him to retreat through the door, but he wanted her to see him. He *needed* her to see him.

He could no longer fight.

To submit might be his undoing, but he'd run mad unless he had her.

He'd been clear regarding Hugo. It was to be all over between them. Whatever hope Geneviève had harbored in that direction would cease. She'd let Hugo down gently. Find herself some other man.

Thinking further ahead was impossible.

She bent one knee, then the other, returning them to a position from which she could rise. Emerging from the water, she stood very still, facing away from him, rivulets of water trickling down her plump, rounded buttocks. Her body was shiny-wet, the elegant curve of her spine arching into her lower back, her delicate waist, and the generous splay of her hips.

All along, she'd known he was there. She'd been taunting him, waiting to see what he would do. He should have known, but what difference would it have made? Almost as soon as he'd entered, he'd abandoned any thought of leaving.

Stepping out, she didn't pick up her towel. Instead, she turned to face him, presenting her body—entirely naked, entirely wet, entirely vulnerable. From the ebony fur at the apex of her thighs to her heavy, tip-tilted breasts, she was every red-blooded man's dream.

Still carrying the sponge from her bath, she held his eyes as she came forward, water dripping from her body. She stroked the sponge upward from her belly, squeezing out its suds upon her right breast, then rubbing its moistness across her nipple. Drawing it away to reveal the constricted peak, she said, "Don't you want to touch me?"

Mallon feared his voice would break. He'd never wanted anything more in his life.

Pulling the towel from his waist, she let it drop to the floor. Looking down, a devilish smile played upon her lips. She brought the sponge to his groin, caressing the length of him with its soapiness, stroking back and forth. A ripple of raw pleasure made his muscles clench. All the while, she kept her head tilted back, looking into his eyes, daring him to take what she offered.

Blood pounding, his control broke, he dragged her to his chest. Bending his head, he took her mouth. No tender meeting of lips but a kiss of all-devouring hunger. Answering in kind, she opened to him, curling her tongue over his.

Dropping the sponge, she wound her arms about his back, clinging to him, moaning as his hands found the lush curve of her bottom—satin-soft and slippery from her bath.

It was just what he'd wished to avoid, a woman having power over him. Power to hurt him. For what if this moment meant nothing to her, while the hunger burning through his soul for her touch and taste meant everything?

How could it have meaning for her when she wanted to marry Hugo?

And then those thoughts melted away, as fire blazed through him.

You've made me want you. At this moment, I have no will. I know only that I must consume you and be consumed.

He was stronger, physically—could have her by force, if he wished, lifting her onto his manhood and taking her pressed against the wall. Her strength was of a different sort. She was tenacious, independent, audacious! Intensely carnal. Luxuriously sensual.

A sound emerged from Mallon's throat more animal than human. He'd never been so swollen with lust, so thick and hard.

The only way to be rid of his obsession was to bed her. Only then would the torment end. And, in the name of all that was holy and unholy, he needed to claim her.

SHE NEEDED HIM INSIDE HER!

To pound away the fire and the yearning. He was everything that Hugo was not, and it was he her body craved. Something unknown whispered her heart desired him, too. From the moment he'd lifted her onto his horse, she'd known. In the library, too, she'd wanted him to ravish her—to cleanse her of Slagsby's foulness through the heat of his passion. The day they'd spent in the cart, she'd been fevered with longing.

Even on the train, she'd known he was unlike any man she'd met before. The attraction between them was more than physical. It was a meeting of souls—made of the same rare mineral, brittle-hard and hidden deep, yet yielding and molten.

And the way he spoke of the moor! She felt his passion and wanted that for herself. She didn't give a rat's arse about the Baroness de Boulainville! Or care a fig for any of those hateful women and priggish, lecherous men. She saw how empty her wishes had been. To think that marriage to Hugo would change anything. She'd been clinging to an illusion, born of her desperation to belong. Château Rosseline had never been hers. Her home—the place in which she might be truly loved —was not in that far off place.

She hoped, she believed, home might be with Lord Wulverton. This evening had confirmed so much. It was Wulverton she must have and she wanted him to yearn for her in the same way. She knew he desired her body, but there was a greater connection than that. She'd seen it in his gaze, something that made her believe if she was his, she'd be cherished, protected, and loved unconditionally. But then, there was also wariness.

His kiss was growing more insistent. His hands claiming her firmly, rolling the tender flesh of her buttock between thumb and forefinger, pinching the underside, making her sigh into his mouth. His manhood was pushing against her belly, the tip moist.

Cupping under her behind, he lifted her. With her thighs clasped around his waist, her slickness found him. She drew breath sharply as the first inches filled her, then yielded slowly to the full length of his penetration.

DEAR GOD, it felt good. Inside her again. He was drowning, with no desire to save himself. Whatever she wanted, he would give her.

Her arms were around his neck and her hands in his

hair. Her eyes were darker than ever, the pupils fully dilated, leaving only a rim of violet.

He groaned as she clenched her inner muscles, driving her hips forward. Holding her arse firmly, he made her follow a rhythm of his choosing. He was almost there, the sweet release only moments away.

Her lips skimmed his neck and downward, to the puckered skin of the scar on his shoulder.

"Yes!" she urged, her breath as ragged as his own. "Oh, Mallon! I love you!"

Mallon's heart lurched and seemed to stop for a moment. The words she'd spoken were a douse of icy water. A slap in the face. It was not simply the fact that, for the first time, she had used his given name. She had made a declaration he had thought he would never hear.

He stopped abruptly, losing his hold upon her. She clung to him for a moment, her arms about his neck and her thighs clutching around his waist, trying to hold on, but the soap on her skin caused her to slither unceremoniously down his body.

Bewildered at finding herself at his feet, she gazed up, frowning in confusion.

No woman had ever said those words—except his mother. The last time he'd heard them had been the day she'd left him, before she rode away to meet the man she loved more.

Geneviève had known him barely a few days. Only hours ago, she'd planned a rendezvous with Hugo! Now, here she was, bouncing on Mallon's member like a three-shilling trollop.

Was that all it had taken for her to reel him in,

making him forget his loyalty to his nephew? A peep show and a few minutes of her skillful touch?

Not that he should be surprised. Since he'd scuppered her pursuit of Hugo, she'd chosen to apply her charms to him instead. Scarred and surly he might be, but he was still a catch, of sorts.

It was just the sort of behavior he expected of women. Not only Geneviève but all of them. Among the whores he'd bedded, love wasn't an emotion, it was a transaction. For his mother, love had been of dubious import, bendable to the caprice of the moment.

Geneviève was kneeling up, extending her arm like a supplicant, her face mere inches from his groin. For a moment, he wondered if she planned to fellate him—as if her caress would erase the chasm between them.

Mallon staggered back, swept by a wave of abhorrence, though more for himself than for her. Bile rose in his throat. All that talk of having Hugo's best interests at heart, and how easily he'd been tempted.

Reeling toward the door, Mallon propelled himself through it, slamming the heavy oak behind him.

CHAPTER TWENTY

THE NIGHT HAD BEEN LONG and terrible. When no more tears had come, she'd tossed in frustration and remorse. She'd taken a gamble, climbing into the bath the maid had drawn for Lord Wulverton, and he'd responded as she'd hoped, as she'd believed he would.

The way he'd kissed her! The way he'd held her so tightly. The look in his eyes as he'd entered her body. It was more than lust. She'd felt the depth of his longing.

But, still, what had possessed her to say those words, to say she loved him! Little wonder he'd recoiled in shock. No one fell in love in the space of a few days. Her heart had been soaring and the words had come tumbling out. She'd meant to say she loved how he made her feel...

She ought to feel angry. She did feel angry—but not just with him. She'd gone about things all the wrong way, and risked losing her chance to make him see how good they could be together.

She wanted him to respond to her with the same

passion she felt, and he'd done so with more intensity than she could have imagined, but, she wanted more than that. She wanted their physical connection to bring them together in other ways. She wanted his respect and his love.

Geneviève sighed. To top it all, she felt wretched. Her head seemed less securely connected than usual, and her throat was sore, alongside the rest of her. At least she wasn't nursing a broken wrist or ankle from coming off the mare yesterday, but she appeared to be coming down with a cold.

There was a knock upon her door.

"Morning, Madam." The girl set down a breakfast tray and went to draw back the curtains. "We'll get the last o' the damp from yer riding habit." She was already laying out the kindling in the grate.

Wrapping the bedspread around her shoulders, Geneviève rose to look out the window. The mist had vanished, burnt off by the rising sun. But frost had taken hold in the night, lacing the trees immediately in front of the inn and the heathland beyond.

She returned to the bed. She couldn't face the eggs or the ham, and the tea didn't smell like any blend with which she was familiar, but it *was* steaming hot.

"I've a note fer ye, from the gentleman." The girl kicked one foot against the other as she took it from her pocket. "The viscount I should say. Him be riding back to the big hall and said he'll send the carriage."

Geneviève felt her stomach turn over. He'd left already? Without waiting? No chance of speaking then

—of explaining what she was feeling. Though who knew where she'd begin.

She waited until the girl had left before opening the envelope. The writing was in a looping hand, and likely more elegant than the inn's stationery saw from one year to the next.

Geneviève,

Last night was a mistake—not just yours, but mine.
I trust you to break off whatever arrangement you've made with Hugo, as gently as you're able.
We need speak no more, nor meet once you've departed Wulverton—as soon as the immediate festivities are over.
The past is best left behind us.

A wave of nausea passed over her. How could he wish her to leave—to walk away without a backward glance?

Merde! Nothing that mattered was acquired easily. Everyone knew that!

She'd seen the grief and resentment he carried with him over his mother. It wasn't the same as her own resentment but it was damnably close. A few years back, Geneviève had made inquiries, wishing to trace the whereabouts of Antoinette Villiers. Her mother had been known throughout Marseille, so discovering her fate hadn't been too great a challenge. Just twelve months after leaving Geneviève at the convent, her death had been recorded in Monte Carlo, from typhus.

There were reports of a love affair with a Russian

prince. The one to place a glittering necklace about her mother's neck, Geneviève supposed.

Mallon's protestations on the fickleness of women were entirely understandable. His mother hadn't just abandoned her husband for her lover, she'd left her children. Little wonder he mistrusted the female sex and the notion of romantic love.

Geneviève had long agreed fondness was possible, and companionship. Physical pleasure, too, with the right man. But love? The sort that bound you to another for a lifetime? That made your heart yearn for a single glance or touch? That left you helpless and vulnerable? Who'd wish such a thing upon themselves?

Could the ecstasy of love ever compensate for love's ability to inflict pain? A week ago, Geneviève would have denied it utterly.

Now, she was ready to fight!

Of course, she needed to speak to Hugo. He didn't deserve to be led any further down the garden path. She'd talk with Beatrice, too. They had as much chance of happiness as any man and woman.

As for Lord Wulverton, more aggressive tactics would be required. Not to deceive him but to inspire him to look anew at what was before him.

Why not let him believe she still pursued Hugo? Make him jealous. He'd come running to prevent the marriage, and to claim her for his own. Might it work?

It would be doubly difficult with bleary eyes and a red nose but, at least, she'd have tried.

Viscount Wulverton might be ready to consign their

passion to the archives but Comtesse Rosseline had other plans!

Geneviève looked out as the carriage ascended, climbing the same hill upon which Hugo had stopped the car. The kiss they'd shared had hardly been a kiss at all—the briefest touching of lips. She felt ashamed, now. How selfish she'd been—but she was determined to set things right.

Below was the prison, where the men would be taking a midday meal, just about now, alone, inside their cells.

She pushed down the window, suddenly anxious to feel the wind and the open air. The moor was looking lovelier than ever, the land falling, rising and falling again, bathed in sunshine yet crisp with frost. It smelled of December, and the promise of snow.

The moor had come to be millions of years before and its grandeur would endure long after she was gone. She, and Lord Wulverton, too. The ardor with which he spoke of the land, its traditions, and its history, was among the things she most admired about him. He knew its wildness, too, and valued it for what it was, in its savage essence.

Before long, they were clattering into the hall's stable-yard. She'd asked the coachman to take her around, rather than dropping her at the front, wishing to check that the bolting horse had made its way back.

There was much bustle, room being made for the

carriages and horses due to arrive that evening. A far grander entertainment was planned than the night before, a proper ball, with twice as many couples, and musicians from Exeter. A cold buffet was also to be laid in the dining room.

Geneviève knew which loose box Artemis was stabled in, and, sure enough, there she was. The mare surveyed Geneviève in a detached manner, continuing her teasing of hay from the rack upon the wall.

"Well, I'm glad you're safe, even if you don't much care the same for me!" said Geneviève. Scarcely had she spoken when there was a rustle from above, where the winter fodder was stacked.

"Hello?" Geneviève went to where the ladder rested, leading into the dark recess beneath the roof. A movement of air lifted some stalks of straw, sending them drifting down through the opening.

Geneviève squinted, peering into the dark, trying to see where the movement came from.

"Can I help ee, Ma'am?"

Geneviève jumped in alarm at the voice which came from behind her. "Oh, Scroggins! How light-footed you are!"

"So folks do say." Scroggins tipped his cap at her. "Light in the saddle, too, I like t'think."

"I'm sure…" Geneviève looked up again. The only sound was from the horses, munching on their feed and pawing their hooves. "I thought I heard something…"

"Up there, Ma'am?" Scroggins shook his head. "No'um has time to be up there today. Like as not, it were a rat. They'um be buggers in the winter… pardon my language, yer ladyship."

"Yes, of course." Geneviève moved away from the ladder, feeling rather foolish.

Scroggins stepped to one side, encouraging her to pass. "An' pardon I for sayin', but it were best if yer didn't come over alone, to the barns and stables and whatnot. The animals can be skittish wi' they'ums they dunnat know."

As Geneviève walked across the stable-yard, she had the distinct feeling she was being watched—and not just by Scroggins.

CHAPTER TWENTY-ONE

"Jolly fortunate you found her!" said Hugo. "Wonder what she was doing up on Fox Tor while the rest of us were enjoying a splendid hunt." He meandered over to the library's drinks cabinet, unstopping a decanter and sniffing gingerly.

Mallon raised an eyebrow. "You noticed she was gone, then? I did wonder if you might be anxious for her."

"Well, yes—of course." Hugo selected one of the lighter-colored single malts, pouring it into two heavy tumblers. "But by the time I realized, the mist was coming down. I just assumed she'd headed back. Then, later on, we got your message that you'd holed up at The Saracen's. Very sensible, although mother seemed a bit miffed that Geneviève didn't make it back for her special luncheon or the dinner. They've become super-friendly, you know—talking *Français* when they think no one is listening. Sharing tips on hats and gloves and bustles and suchlike, I expect. Rather nice for mother to have a compatriot to chat with."

"Hmm." Mallon took the glass from his nephew.

"To be honest, I was more upset about Slagsby," Hugo admitted. "I didn't even know he was gone until he didn't appear for dinner. He's never liked horses, so it was no surprise he didn't bother with the hunt." Hugo went to look out the window, as if doing so might summon back his friend. "Set off in his motor without saying goodbye…and he'd promised to take me for a spin. We used to rub along well enough at Eton, and he said he couldn't face Christmas in Northumbria with his own family. Don't think they get on too well."

"Perhaps for the best he's headed off. I wasn't too enamoured of him, myself." Though Hugo seemed genuinely upset, news of Slagsby's departure was music to Mallon's ears. "I've meant to ask, what are your plans?"

He watched as Hugo took a tentative sip from his glass. Mallon knew full well his nephew didn't enjoy spirits. Hugo was far too honest-faced to hide his reactions. Like so many young men, he thought feigning a taste for whisky would make him appear more mature, much like growing a moustache—something that would be a few years off yet for Hugo, whose chin was as smooth as a baby's.

"Well, I might go for another ride. I do love a good gallop. And I suppose I'd better stir myself to wrap a few gifts." He gave an apologetic grin. "Nothing too exciting, mind you. Bit limited in the choices hereabouts."

"That's marvellous, Hugo, but I was thinking rather longer term." Mallon inwardly rolled his eyes, and reminded himself to be patient. The matter of Hugo's future was a conversation long overdue. He didn't even know, for sure, how attached his nephew had grown to the countess.

"Oh, right. Got you!" Hugo assumed a more serious expression. "Might go and survey the inheritance. Those vineyards, you know. Mother seems eager, although there's no need for me to be involved in actually running the place. The vintners have all that in hand, thank goodness. Don't need the likes of me interfering!" Hugo gave a bark of laughter. "But wouldn't do any harm to show my face, would it? Let them see the new lord of the manor…or should that be château?"

"Yes, that's an idea." Mallon gave a smile of encouragement. "A man should see a little of the world."

"Just my thinking," said Hugo. "Although my *Français* is a bit rusty. Wasn't even that good when I was at school…"

"Not to worry. It will all work out, I'm sure." Mallon shifted in his seat. "I realize your uncle's death has brought you a title and lands of your own, but you know Wulverton Hall will also be yours one day, and the viscountcy."

"Seems rather rum, doesn't it?" Hugo looked wistful. "So many chaps without much of a fortune at all, and two falling in my lap without me having to lift a finger."

Mallon nodded. It was 'rum', the way things worked out. Mallon might have wished for a more resolute streak in the young man who would, one day, inherit

Wulverton and all its lands, but it could have been far worse. Hugo's heart was in the right place, even if he was limited in the brains department. Mallon had grown quite fond of him. He had Edward's manner all right, taking the world as it came and generally seeing the best in it.

He wondered what Allenby de Wolfe would have made of it all, or the great Gaetan de Wolfe. Hugo hardly fitted the heroic mold of their de Wolfe ancestors.

But then, neither do I, thought Mallon. He'd done his duty as a soldier, it was true, but he'd never considered himself brave. No more than any other man, at least. As for honor and acclaim, Mallon had no desire for either. He'd be content to do right by his tenants and to ensure the security of the Wulverton estate for future generations. Having no son of his own, he needed Hugo for that.

And Hugo needed him, too.

Just over two years had passed since Edward had died, and Hugo appeared to be dealing well with his bereavement, but he needed a father-figure to guide him.

Mallon hadn't yet processed his feelings of grief over his brother's death. It was another emotion he'd battened down, unwilling to dwell upon what he'd lost. What point was there in rehashing the past? Better to concentrate on what he could do now, to make amends.

Naturally, the subject of Hugo, one day, taking a wife, ought to be brought up.

Mallon took a deep breath. "The fact is, it falls to

you, Hugo, as the future viscount, to ensure the succession." Seeing a look of confusion cross his nephew's face, Mallon elaborated further. "Stallion and well-bred mare, Hugo, and a stable full of healthy foals."

Hugo colored a little, as realization dawned. "Ram and ewes, birds and bees?"

"Exactly." Mallon suppressed a sigh.

"Well, I'd not thought to marry just yet." Hugo swirled the whisky around his glass. "But I *have* been wondering what it might be like, just lately..."

Mallon gave a tight smile. What he said next needed to be worded carefully. "Hugo, it goes without saying that the mother of all those...foals, should be a woman worthy of being brought into the family."

"Someone of rank, you mean?" Hugo nodded. "You intend for me to go up for the Season and choose my filly." He looked pleased with himself. "I'm well ahead of you on that count."

Mallon sat further back in his chair. At last, they were getting somewhere. "Rank isn't everything, Hugo, nor is wealth."

"That's what I've always thought, too. Beatrice, for instance! Lovely girl! Not a penny to her name and no nobility to speak of, although I believe her grandfather on her father's side was the youngest son of a baronet somewhere in Somerset." Hugo gave a low whistle. "I've always been sweet on her. Used to play together as children. Lovely girl, most certainly."

Hugo looked out of the window again, in the vague direction of the Wapshots' rectory, requiring Mallon to cough loudly to regain his attention.

"Sorry!" Hugo gave another grin. "Just remembering." He gave his head a little shake. "As I say, I'd not been thinking of the wedded state, but I must own to my heart having been set aflutter, and by a woman perfect on all counts." He tapped the side of his nose in conspiratorial fashion.

"Oh, yes?" Mallon spoke through clenched teeth.

"She has funds of her own, so she can't possibly be after me for mine." Hugo gave a guffaw. "But, more than that, she's the epitome of feminine refinement. Bearing of a queen! Figure of a goddess!" He sat forward in excitement. "And, she rather likes me. We've even kissed…just a little."

"I see." Mallon felt himself grow cold.

"Nothing to jeopardize her reputation," Hugo added quickly. "Just a peck, really, although I must be a pretty good kisser, as she seemed to want me to carry on." His cheeks heated again.

Mallon steeled himself to say what must be said. "I've no doubt that she does want you to kiss her, Hugo, and a great many things besides." Mallon gave Hugo a pointed look. "I'm guessing you're referring to the countess."

Hugo nodded vigorously, his color deepening.

"You must remember she's a woman of experience."

Hugo tugged at his collar, his eyes growing wide. "She's been married before, so she'll know what's what, I suppose." His expression veered from wonderment to fright and settled somewhere in the realm of awe.

Mallon inwardly cursed himself. Hugo, he should

have realized, had never slept with a woman. Goodness only knows what fantasies were now being kindled.

"Let me be plain, Hugo. The countess may only be a few years your senior but she will have enjoyed...vastly different experiences." Mallon meant to offer warning, but Hugo was sitting on the edge of his seat, apparently eager to hear more.

Mallon cleared his throat, taking a sterner tone. "I suspect she has a number of men among her acquaintance."

"Golly!" Hugo appeared to be finding it hard to catch his breath. "And of all those male admirers, she's keen on me!" He rose unsteadily. "I know that a woman only lets you kiss her when she's pretty serious, but it hadn't occurred to me how far the countess must love me. To choose me above all those other chaps, I mean."

He appeared to be in a daze. "So much to think about, and I haven't even acquired a ring. Better take myself to the jewellers in Exeter, unless mother has a ring she might give me for the purpose..." He was mumbling to himself now, considering the logistics of the proposal.

Mallon watched, incredulous, as his nephew made his way to the door.

"Thank you, Uncle. Without your counsel, I mightn't have realized. I'll make sure to waste no time."

As the door clicked shut behind young Hugo, Mallon let forth a torrent of curses. So much for his handling the matter with delicacy. He'd achieved nothing but to set his nephew further on the path to ruin. The notion of him living happily ever after with Geneviève was laughable.

He could see it now, the marriage ending in scandal and everlasting doubt over the children's bloodline. He'd never permit it!

Geneviève was a law unto herself. She'd say anything —do anything—to get what she wanted. Last night had only confirmed that. Believing that her plans to ensnare Hugo had been foiled, she'd thrown herself at the second most enticing option.

Mallon took up his glass of whisky. Savoring the aroma, he battled the temptation to gulp it down. It was hard for him to think about Geneviève without growing angry. Harder still to think of her without growing hard! When she'd stepped out of the bath, he'd been transfixed. *Sweet Jesus and all the angels!* If he never lay with another woman again, he'd at least have that memory to take to his grave.

Of course, she'd not meant what she said. Her— loving him! He doubted she could love anyone. The look of perplexity when he'd shied away from her had been acting, hadn't it? And the way her eyes had pleaded as she'd looked up from where he'd dropped her to the floor?

Mallon sank his head into his hands. How big a fool had he been? *Hell's teeth!* How could he have been so blind!

The thought of her with Hugo riled him not just for the unsuitability of the match. He knew bloody well why he couldn't bear the thought of it. He didn't want to imagine Geneviève with another man, with Hugo or with anyone else; and there was only one reason for that!

The revelation of it struck him like the lightning upon Saul on the road to Damascus. She did care for him, and he, God help him, was utterly, burningly, blindingly infatuated with her. He wanted to explore what was growing between them, and to get to know everything about her.

Through the heat of the Afghan desert and the blazing summers of Constantinople, he'd lived in perpetual winter. Returning to Dartmoor, he'd told himself it would be enough to undertake the duties of his title. And yet, he was tired of being alone, of proclaiming he needed no one.

Mallon passed his whisky from one hand to the other. His tongue ached for the familiar burn, for the ginger fire of the alcohol and its sweet oblivion. He need only bring it to his lips.

Hell and damnation!

Resolutely, Mallon placed his whisky glass on the side table. It had taken all this time to find her. One way or another, he'd discover a way to make her his.

CHAPTER TWENTY-TWO

As Mallon entered the corridor leading to Geneviève's room, he happened upon her maid, loitering as if unsure of herself, but stirred to action as he appeared.

"*Excusez moi*, my lord." She bobbed a curtsey, pressing herself to the wall as he drew near. She appeared unnerved, unwilling to meet his eyes. In her hand, quite clearly, she held a pale lilac envelope, and he could read the name upon it without difficulty—that of Hugo!

"A note from your mistress?" It was a statement more than a question.

The girl tried to hide the thing behind her back, but Mallon was not to be deflected.

"Permit me to take it for you."

"*Mais, non! Je ne peux pas!*"

She attempted to dart past, obliging him to clasp her arm and pull it from her grasp. Despite her desperate clutching, he wrenched it free. Pale with fright, she sobbed and scurried away.

It gave Mallon no pleasure to treat her so but, knowing the content of the last note Geneviève had written, he was determined to read this one.

It took but a moment to scan the message.

My Darling Hugo
We must speak privately. Come to my room with all haste.
Geneviève

Mallon's fury rose on seeing the words. He'd been coming to her in good faith, wishing to apologize for having fled the night before. It was not the idea of love that terrified him but the power it would give another over his heart—the ability to betray and crush. He'd been willing to take that leap for Geneviève, by letting her into the place he'd kept guarded.

Now, he saw she was up to her old tricks, undeterred from her goal. The profession of love she'd offered the night before meant nothing. This was her solution to having her hand forced. She intended to compromise Hugo utterly and extract his proposal as a consequence.

He'd been right to be wary. What a performance she'd given at the inn! She'd almost convinced him that she harbored true feelings. It had all been a lie.

Reaching her door, he gave a cursory knock before pushing it open. She was upon the far side of the room, gazing into the fire, her long hair hanging loosely down her back.

He swallowed.

She wore nothing but a gossamer-light peignoir. With the firelight behind her, the gauzy fabric was utterly transparent. Despite his anger, Mallon was rendered mute by the lush curve of her bottom. There was no fighting the familiar ache in his groin.

"My love," she whispered. "I knew you'd come." As she turned, her face expressed surprise, then a flash of irritation, before her features settled into an audacious air.

The revealing gown was clearly for Hugo's benefit. Facing him, she gave Mallon a tantalizing view of the swell of her breasts, the curve of her hip, and the lush, dark curls between her legs.

Mallon's blood ran hot. He'd teach her what it meant to trifle with a man's passion. It would take no time to cover the distance between them and tear the delicate gown from her shoulders. If she screamed, he'd smother it with a kiss, but he knew she'd neither scream nor pull away. He'd only to grasp her firmly about those hips, and she'd be his, her warmth about him as he drove full hilt.

Even as he fought the urge, she padded barefoot toward him, a look of challenge in her eye.

"It seems you cannot keep away, Lord Wulverton." She was standing improperly close, as if daring him to lay hands upon her.

"You seek something from me?" Her eyes lowered to the tailored fit of his trousers, the tightness of which permitted no concealment of his desire.

Despite all her games, his craving for her was undeniable, but he could not abase himself. To declare his need for her or make any declaration of feeling, would be to place himself in her power.

"I do." He gritted his teeth, unable to utter what had been in his heart. "I thought you'd see reason, but apparently not." He held up the note, written in her hand, before tossing it away. "I demand you abandon your pursuit of Hugo."

"After all my efforts?" she arched her brow. "I could only consider such a retreat if there were compensation..." She tilted back her head as she spoke, her lips tauntingly close, her fingers touching lightly upon his shirt.

The desire to bury his mouth upon hers and pull her ripeness into his arms threatened to overwhelm him, but to do so would bring him right back to where he'd begun. He thirsted for her, yes, but on his terms.

"I was unaware you were in need of funds, Madam," he spoke coldly, fully cognizant that it wasn't money she sought.

"You know what I want." Her voice was low and husky. "And I know why you're really here." Her fingers were inching down, and he had no will to stop her.

"You wish me for yourself." Deftly, she opened the first two buttons of his trousers. A few more moments and her hand would release him. "Hugo has kissed me, nothing more."

At the mention of Hugo's name, Mallon's anger surged again. How easy it was for her! Had she no feeling!

He grabbed her wrist, and Geneviève gave a strangled cry but struggled only for a moment. Making herself limp, she raised her face to him with eyes half closed, offering him the fullness of her lips.

"Go to blazes!" he hissed, gently pushing her away.

Rubbing her wrist, she gave a perverse smile. "If you wish to hold my hand so badly, my lord, I'll save you a dance at tonight's ball. Hugo shall want most of my time, naturally, but I may spare you one turn about the room."

"Believe me, Madam, I will prevent this match." Mallon's voice held a threatening growl. "I shall stop you, by whatever means. You may remain here until Twelfth Night, after which you may carry yourself to London and screw the entire male population of the capital, from frill-shirted footmen to the hammer-fisted butchers of Smithfields, but I *will* have your promise to cease pursuit of my nephew."

She appeared to flinch, but only for a moment. The next, she was again composed, and merely mouthed the words, knowing his eyes were fixed upon her lips. *Make me!*

In one great stride, he reached her, lifting her in a single sweep, one arm beneath the crook of her knee and the other about her back. Even before they arrived at the bed, his mouth was ravaging her. She gasped his name, but he swallowed it in the ferociousness of his kiss.

Throwing her down into the soft mattress, he towered above, his heart hammering wildly. She bit her lips where he'd kissed her, licking where she could still taste him. She smiled wickedly, then quivered as he grasped her breast through the sheer fabric of her gown. Three buttons on his trousers remained closed, constraining his girth. Despite the discomfort, he left them fastened; he was still in possession of himself, albeit by a thread.

Tipping back her chin, she invited his mouth, pulling his tongue inside, sucking on the tip, drawing him down to her, sighing with the weight of his body on hers.

God! It would be so easy! He was straining for her, aching at the thought of what he might do. She wriggled beneath him while taking his kiss deeper.

She tasted of sin.

Kissing her prevented him from thinking properly. He wanted to slide into her and keep thrusting until they were both gasping with need.

It required all his self-control to peel himself away.

"Do you accept my terms, Madam?"

"I might," she conceded, her mouth curving in a feline smile. "But I need more persuading…as to my compensation."

"You might, or you will?"

"Tell me what I want to hear and I'll behave impeccably." She curved upward, pressing herself to him. "I want to hear you desire me. That you cannot bear the thought of another having me. You cannot admit it, but your heart will ache for me when I'm gone! You need love, Mallon, as much as any man! Even though you fear love will be snatched away as soon as it's given, you cannot live without belief in a kindred soul to tarry with you through this life."

In response, he grasped a handful of her hair, tumbled loose across the pillow, wrapping its length about this fist, causing her to catch her breath.

How dare she assume to know him, or the hidden yearnings of his heart! How dare she tell him what he felt!

Except that she was right on every count. She'd seen through his blood and bone to the fear clutched cold about his heart. Looking into the depths of her eyes, he saw no hint of taunting—only the sincerity of one whose own happiness lay in the answer he would give.

He relaxed his hold upon her hair—her dark curls, so soft and luxuriant—but kept her beneath him. He needed to maintain the upper hand, yet a tendril of hope unfurled within him.

"Your ring on my finger, Lord Wulverton…" Her voice was a whisper. "Your jousting lance, wherever you choose to put it…"

He suppressed a groan at hearing her offer herself so crudely.

Her lips curled in a knowing smile. "And my promise I'll let Hugo down gently."

She arched against him, the chiffon pulling tight against her breasts. Unable to resist, he kissed down her neck, pushing aside the fabric of her gown until he found the soft swell of her flesh. He took the nipple between his teeth, pulling it hard into the warmth of his mouth. She was trembling with desire, fervent, willing —a voluptuous goddess and a scarlet vixen. Never before had a woman's sounds of pleasure stirred him so profoundly.

"We may put the former on account," she gasped, breathless, "and deal with the second and third on the list this very evening."

His manhood, summoned by her oath, reminded him that it had already decided to accept, but his head told him not to trust her.

Whatever promises she made, he would not rely upon them this evening. Hugo was far too caught up in romantic ideas to hear her rejection tonight. He'd be inclined to think her charmingly modest—for weren't all virtuous women supposed to refuse a first proposal and require further pursuit. The outcome of such games was too uncertain.

There was only one thing for it.

Slowly, he drew out the ivory ribbon gathering the yoke of her gown then, raising her arm, wrapped the satin around her wrist.

"Whatever you're doing, I think I like it," she murmured, lying still as he stretched out her other slender limb, securing both together, pulled taut above her head. Kneeling above her, he freed the long sash from her waist and looped it through the bindings on her wrists before fastening it to the wolf's head carved into the center of the headboard.

"Helpless and at your mercy," she purred.

Bound as she was, her arms held taut by the satin ribbons, she could not escape. Satisfied, he rose from the bed, adjusting his trousers and pulling down his jacket to cover what bulged between his legs.

She looked at him in some alarm. "Shouldn't those things be coming off?" Then, "Where are you going?"

"We'll see about those terms later, my love. The last of them, I think, may be best put off until tomorrow."

Reaching for the quilt, he pulled it over her. "I'll be back before midnight."

As he locked the door, he heard her sneeze and curse him—in English and French, and in the most exquisite detail.

CHAPTER TWENTY-THREE

THE SUPPER HAD SEEMED to last an eternity, the chatter about him mere noise. Marguerite had arranged for some rollicking mummery, their farmworkers appearing in garish masks and costumes before partaking of the wassail punchbowl. It was the sort of folk custom he'd once enjoyed, cheering St. George's slaying of the dragon, and the outrageous prancing of the hobbyhorse. He believed in upholding those traditions but, this evening, he'd been in no mood for the teasing jokes and boisterous cavorting.

Moreover, the actors had enjoyed several glasses too many, resulting in considerable effort to remove them. The clock had long since chimed eleven.

There were few families Lady Marguerite felt worthy of her invitation, but she'd cast her net wide to the grander houses on the outskirts of the moor, to Tavistock and Yelverton, Ashburton and Bovey Tracey, to ensure enough couples for a ball.

For Mallon, it had been a trial to be endured. A

room full of noisy and self-satisfied guests congratulating themselves on their wealth and taste and breeding. How frivolous they were!

Though who am I to talk? What have I to show for all these years of life?

He'd informed Lisette her mistress had a migraine and wished not to be disturbed, then relayed the same message to Marguerite. She offered cursory sympathies, for she had far too much to organize to dwell on Geneviève's absence.

Only Hugo had seemed genuinely downhearted at the countess keeping to her room.

"Rotten to be missing all the fun. Might I go up do you think and take her a little something?"

"Best not," Mallon had declared firmly. "Migraines are terrible things." He'd steered Hugo firmly toward Beatrice. "Mustn't neglect your other guests, Hugo. Not many people here of your age, so you'd do well to keep her company. We've the fiddlers for music, so nothing to stop you from taking her onto the floor. Your mother's a tyrant, making the poor girl play all the time."

To Mallon's relief, Hugo had adopted the idea in perfect contentment.

Throughout the evening, Mallon had been aware of the key within his pocket, and the delicious Geneviève recumbent on her bed. He'd lingered in the passageway at first, wishing to see if she'd call out. Though the walls and doors were thick in that part of the house, a scream would be heard.

However, she'd kept quiet. He'd made her as comfortable as possible, placing a second pillow behind her head on which to rest her elbows, and the ribbons were not too tightly wound. Nevertheless, after several hours, he feared her shoulders would be aching.

The anger which had consumed him earlier had ebbed. Hugo, it appeared, was most amenable to being distracted. Mallon needed no further proof that his nephew's heart would recover from Geneviève's rejection. Moreover, it had taken less than an hour for Mallon to realize that it was Geneviève's absence that made the festivities so dull.

Resist as he might try, he was disastrously besotted, and it was too sodding late to get a grip on himself. Far too late and bloody inconvenient.

Whatever he pretended, he didn't just want an illicit liaison; he wanted to share a life. The thought of facing a future without Geneviève—at Wulverton, or anywhere else, was too desolate to contemplate.

WHEN HE RETURNED, she was asleep, her chest rising and falling in slumber. She snuffled and sniffed and shifted slightly, her body restricted by his handiwork. He wondered what she was dreaming about. Knowing Geneviève, something wicked!

Delivering her from her constraints, he lowered his lips to her wrists, turning each to seek out the delicate skin above her pulse, before drawing down her arms to rest by her sides.

She was so very beautiful.

The quilt had slithered down, revealing the curve of

her breasts through the sheer fabric. She was peaches and cream waiting to be eaten.

He couldn't help himself. If he was gentle, she wouldn't wake. He pulled back the covers, placing his hand lightly on her hip. She was remarkably warm. She mumbled something but did not stir.

He lowered to her breast, breathing hot through the thin chiffon. So soft! He closed his mouth about that softness, kissing her nipple. He cupped the other, offering a gentle caress.

She shifted, parting her legs, but he knew that this was where he should stop. He wanted to trace and touch every part of her, to kiss and taste and learn, but he knew he should leave. To act as he wished without her consent would be a violation. Moreover, if she were honest in her proposal that they wed, they'd have a life-time to enjoy each other.

He drew back to the edge of the bed, regretful but knowing that he did what was right. She'd been willing enough a few hours ago but that had been before he'd left her tied up for the evening.

He'd behaved abominably and, when she woke, he'd have to face her wrath. But he wished to be close to her, with nothing between them—to be naked, her skin against his.

Having removed his clothes, he climbed beneath the quilt. The air smelt sweetly of her. Mallon's conscience was turning somersaults as she twisted toward him, her foot nudging his.

Damn it! He was only flesh and blood!

She moaned as he drew his hand lower, pushing up

her gown to reveal her bare thighs. He lowered his lips to Geneviève's belly and she shivered, uttering the smallest of sighs.

"Don't stop," she breathed, and a rush of joy filled him. He brushed his face in her soft curls, inhaling her fragrance, then parted the plump folds, caressing her in one long, languid stroke, coming to rest on her swollen pearl. She whimpered as he teased it with his tongue's tip, then sucked upon its velvet, delighting in each sound she made.

LISETTE HAD BEEN reluctant to wait in the corridor for Lord Wulverton's approach, but Geneviève had known he'd pass eventually. Her maid had clearly acted her part effectively, for he'd entered in such a fury, convinced of her duplicity!

Seeing he meant to restrain her, she'd hardly been able to curb her excitement—but then he'd made his exit, just as things had begun to be interesting.

It had taken a great deal of patience to wait, though the ties were not uncomfortable. He'd positioned her carefully, supporting her arms atop the pillows. Had she wished to free herself, she might have done so with her teeth, but she was content to wait. When he returned, she knew, he'd be unable to resist her.

She'd drowsed for a while but heard the click of the key in the lock. Time to be still and await what she knew to be inevitable.

Would his lovemaking be a savage demonstration of

his strength? His will over hers? The thought of Lord Wulverton claiming her as she struggled excited her, though any resistance on her part would be purely feigned.

As he nuzzled her breasts, it was torture not to speak. A tickle in her nose almost caused her to sneeze, but she'd managed to convince him that she was sleeping, she was sure.

He smelt of cologne and brandy and cigar smoke, and of male arousal. By the time he removed his clothes, she was quivering with anticipation.

When his tongue entered, she was unable to curb her need, writhing against its flickering demands until she was keening. Clutching his head, she urged him deeper, arching to meet his mouth, repeating his name. She cried 'Oh! And 'Yes!' and begged 'Please!' as he worshipped her, until she was tugged into fluttering ecstasy, breaking wave upon wave.

"Geneviève!" His kisses trailed from her throat toward her ear. "My Geneviève."

He kissed her with the passion of one who had waited too long for such comfort. He would kiss her everywhere, bringing her more pleasure than she could imagine. When he released her mouth, he returned to her breasts, pushing down the chiffon to reveal her satin smoothness. They were exquisite. He would never tire of teasing those cherry nipples, licking first one then the other, murmuring his delight in her body.

Soon, she was begging again, shifting her hips to seek out his manhood, offering him her slipperiness.

"Not yet." He knew he must slow down or spill immediately.

"Then let me taste you."

"I shan't last," he warned, but she urged her request again.

"Here," she commanded, licking her lips.

Holding the headboard, he lowered his thickness to her open mouth, gasping his astonishment as she drew him down, humming against his length.

Dear God! He was conquered. His body was hers.

He held himself above her, letting her choose the depth of her strokes. He'd known it was impossible to resist.

Within moments, his seed was rising, and with a wild cry, he surrendered.

CHAPTER TWENTY-FOUR

THEY RESTED in each other's arms, whispering all the things they'd not yet said—all the things they'd never said before.

Then, they fell to kissing again, which led to limbs entwined, and she was silken wet, her body pleading for more of him.

He began slowly, relishing her squeezing of him, inch by inch, as he entered her warmth. He growled with pleasure, but soon it was she who was trembling, wanting him buried to the hilt.

"Deeper! Please!"

She'd never desired a man like this. Never wanted someone to have such control over her, but she knew Mallon's pain and his need, his weakness and vulnerability. In return, she wanted to give him everything. She wanted to know him and for him to know her.

At her urging, he pinned her down, joining her in the hungry race toward rapture. When it came, she arched to meet it, vaguely aware of his body tensing, of labored breath and his final thrust, locked together as she let go, giving herself to the flashing darkness of her climax, spinning her into the abyss.

Afterward, she asked him to stay, wanting to feel his chest against her back as she drifted to sleep. Listening to his steady breathing beside her, she realized she was truly happy. Mallon needed her love just as she needed his, and the only thing she really wanted was to give that love to him, and prove herself worthy of his in return.

It was time to banish the spectres and begin a new life together. First, she had to speak to Hugo. She'd been cruel, leading him on, but she could put things right.

Geneviève was careful to lock the drawing room door. The last thing she needed was an interruption. The dogs trotted in behind, making an immediate circuit around each chair and a second sweep of the perimeter—no doubt, in search of crumbs.

Outside, the sky was starkly white, the window panes frosted across each corner where the sun was yet to touch. Fortunately, the fire had been blazing for some time, making the room quite cosy.

She decided not to beat around the bush.

"I hold you in the highest affection, Hugo, but I fear I must step back, discovering that another holds a prior claim."

Hugo looked most put out. "A prior claim? Dash it, Geneviève! What do you mean? I'm no philanderer!

Barely know how to talk to a woman, come to that. It wasn't until you showed up that I realized what all this romance malarkey was about!"

Geneviève kept an arm's length between herself and Hugo, lest he take a sudden notion to prove himself with a kiss.

"No one could accuse you of the least impropriety," Geneviève asserted. "But, I think you underestimate your charm, Hugo dear. For there is one whose love for you is of long-standing. She holds such deep regard I fear it would break her heart were I to continue our courtship."

Hugo looked utterly baffled.

"You wouldn't *want* to break a woman's heart, would you Hugo?"

"Well, of course not! But how's a chap to navigate all this love-business when he hasn't a clue who's taken a fancy to him." He rubbed his forehead.

"I hardly like to interfere…" Geneviève crossed her fingers behind her back. If she *was* employing some deceit, she hoped the angels would forgive her, it being in a good cause. "Perhaps, I could tell you, if you really do need my help…"

"I wish you would!" declared Hugo, shaking his head in puzzlement. "For I can't imagine who you're talking about…unless it's the girl in the post office in Prince-town. She's quite pretty, you know, and always very friendly." He looked suddenly alarmed. "But I swear I've only ever asked her for stamps!"

"No, no!" Geneviève coughed to suppress her laughter. "The lady in question is far more intimately connected with you Hugo. Can you truly not guess?"

"Intimately connected?" Hugo blinked rapidly, clearly riffling his mental list of possible female candidates. "Not Mrs. Wapshot's spinster cousin!" An expression of horror overcame him.

"Hugo!" Geneviève was, at last, obliged to be stern. "The woman of whom I speak is quite your own age and suitable in every way, as far as I can make out. It's Beatrice, Hugo! Beatrice!"

Hugo's mouth opened and closed several times without any sound emerging. Finally, he gulped. "Well, that's rather better than Mrs. Wapshot's cousin—or the girl in the post office."

"Yes, it is." Geneviève allowed herself a broad smile. "Had you really no inkling? Haven't you seen how she looks at you? Like a princess who's sighted her prince over a garden wall but isn't quite sure how to jump over."

"Perhaps. Sometimes. Just now and then." Hugo tugged on his ear. "I look at her, too. We've known each other forever. I never thought it meant anything."

Geneviève ventured to put a hand on Hugo's arm. "I'm all for seizing the day. Now you know she's your true match, you mustn't waste time. I wouldn't even tell your mother, if I were you. Drive over to Beatrice today and make your proposal. It will be such a surprise for everyone. Just think what pleasure you'll be bringing both your families! The most wonderful Christmas gift of all! And I wouldn't hang about with a long engagement, either. Show Beatrice that you're all in by setting the date as soon as possible."

"By Jove!" Hugo was almost bouncing from foot to foot. "I can't thank you enough. He grasped her in a firm handshake, beaming with excitement. "And jolly decent of you to let me know, what with us having begun our grand passion." He looked suddenly sheepish. "I do hope this won't cause you too much unhappiness, knowing we won't be together after all."

"How could I stand in the way of two people so obviously meant for each other?" Geneviève extracted her hand, discreetly giving it a reviving rub.

"I wonder if it's too late to drive into Exeter for a ring…" Hugo squinted at the clock on the mantel. He seemed to have taken Geneviève's suggestion very much to heart.

"Ah!" Geneviève gave a satisfied smile. It was certainly a relief to have the concluding part of her plan presented so naturally. "There, I can help."

She drew out a blue velvet box from her pocket.

"This is yours, left to you by your grandmother. In the Rosseline family for generations, Hugo, and now passing to you."

Opening the lid, he made a noise not unlike that uttered by Geneviève herself on first seeing the perfectly crafted jewel.

"What a beauty!" Hugo held it up, the square-cut diamond sparkling in its delicate silver setting.

"Naturally, your bride should also have the matching pieces." Geneviève had thought long and hard about parting with the jewels Maxim had given her, but she knew it would be unjust to keep them. "I've laid them out on my dressing table for you."

"Well, I never!" gasped Hugo. He was about to say something else, but before he had the chance, he lost his grasp on the ring. With a bark of alarm, he watched it roll, disappearing beneath one of the smaller tables.

Falling to the floor, he began skimming the carpet with his palms. Seeing their master in prone position and hopeful of a game, Muffin landed his huge paws on Hugo's shoulders while Tootle let forth a full-throated howl.

"Silly dogs! Down! Off me, I say!"

Geneviève had a strange feeling of *déjà vu*. Not the sight of Hugo rummaging under the sofa but something else she couldn't quite put her finger on.

"Got it!" Hugo sat up, holding the ring aloft. "Wouldn't have done for one of the dogs to have swallowed it!"

"Well, it would have pushed back your plans by a few days," Geneviève conceded.

"Here, let me help you up." She reached down, offering Hugo a steadying hand. Rising, he gave her a swift kiss on the cheek.

"Thank you, Aunt Geneviève, and I do hope you'll be here for the wedding.

"Mais bien sûr!"

Geneviève wrapped Hugo in a hug. She was delighted it wouldn't be she walking down the aisle with the young lord. Far better she become his aunt through another connection altogether.

It really was turning out to be the most marvellous Christmas.

THE EVENTS of the previous night still seemed unreal, as if he'd dreamt all that happiness, and Mallon had been on tenterhooks all morning.

It appeared only proper to depart Geneviève's bedchamber before the rest of the household stirred. If he'd had his way, he'd have remained under the covers with her all day, and the next, right through until the new year. Withers could have brought periodic trays of sustenance. Everyone else could do as they liked!

However, Geneviève had insisted they do things properly.

She'd promised to speak to Hugo today, but he was nervous. Everything had happened so suddenly. What if she had a change of heart?

From the turn in the stairs, he'd seen her take Hugo into the drawing room. Looking at his watch, he'd noted the hour and the minute. How long would it take? The grandfather clock chimed eleven and then quarter past.

What could they be doing? Wasn't it a simple matter?

Perhaps not. Hugo had surely never been in love before. His heart might be in pieces. Geneviève might be required to comfort him.

Mallon took several deep breaths.

Once Hugo had her in his arms, he might be tempted to kiss her.

Mallon rubbed his eyebrow.

Geneviève might, for form's sake, respond, to avoid hurting Hugo's feelings, but just a farewell kiss.

It would be fine.

Mallon paced the landing, looked out the window, then paced some more.

It was here that he'd smashed that blighter Slagsby on the nose. There was still a slight stain on the carpet where the blood had gushed. Not too visible among the burgundy patterning, but Mallon could see it. What had been going on that night? He'd never asked, and Geneviève hadn't volunteered the information.

Not that he required the full story. Of course not. It was pretty apparent she wasn't willing, and the bastard was forcing himself on her. What else did Mallon need to know? Perhaps why they'd both been on the landing in the first place at that time of night, and Geneviève in her nightclothes?

Mallon shook away the thought. He shouldn't be so suspicious. Geneviève was not his mother. She had a healthy appetite in bedroom matters, that was sure, but she'd declared her feelings for him most unequivocally, as they'd basked in the afterglow of the most wonderful of couplings.

He understood her now; and she understood him. They were going to thumb their noses at the world and marry as soon as possible.

Geneviève didn't need anyone else. She was in love with him.

And yet, Mallon couldn't help but worry.

Taking the stairs double-quick, he laid his hand on the doorknob to the drawing room. He'd just pop his head in. The main business would be over by now, wouldn't it? He might offer Hugo his shoulder or a word of advice. Whatever was needed.

He turned the handle, only to find that the door wouldn't open. Someone had locked it. Someone didn't want him to come in—or anyone else.

The muscles in his neck tensed. There was nothing to be concerned about, was there? No need to check up on them? Mallon merely wished to know how things were going…and it was somewhat galling to be locked out. He held his ear to the door but could hear nothing beyond the murmur of voices. That was something, at least. A fellow couldn't get up to much while maintaining a steady conversation.

He considered, briefly, going outside to peer through the window but chastised himself immediately. He was turning over a new leaf, allowing himself to give his trust. Without that, what sort of man would he be?

Nevertheless, he could do with some air. It might calm his nerves and stop him from dwelling on these wayward thoughts.

IT WAS DAMNABLY cold with a fine sleet falling, and Mallon immediately regretted not having grabbed his coat. All those years in the Arabias had made him soft!

These moorland winters would take some getting used to again.

He'd take a turn about the immediate grounds. As long as he walked briskly, he'd avoid becoming too chilled.

With breath pluming, Mallon came around the corner and was surprised to see the butler's shuffling form disappearing into the stables. Following the social whirl of the past few days, Marguerite had given most of the staff a few hours off before they began preparations for the carolling of Christmas Eve and the lighting of the Yule Log.

It seemed most strange that Withers would spend that precious time outside in the cold. Mallon could think of no reason for him to be frequenting horse boxes. Was the old chap losing his marbles, wandering about without knowing what he was doing? If Withers was off his rocker, Mallon would need to intervene before he hurt himself.

Entering the stables, Mallon was relieved at how much warmer it was. Horses were hot-blooded beasties, and the boxes were well insulated against the winter bite. As Mallon walked further in, six equine faces popped into view, looking for a nose rub or a carrot, or anything else that might be on offer.

Perhaps Withers wasn't so mad. There were worse places to escape to, after all. Mallon made a mental note to retreat out here next time he was feeling exasperated or if he needed to retreat from one of Marguerite's tea parties.

Strangely, Withers was nowhere to be seen. Mallon

checked each stall and found no sign. However, approaching the far end, he noticed the rungs of the hayloft ladder were mud-smeared and slightly wet. Someone had been climbing up, and very recently.

Mallon stared into the gaping recess above.

He thought he heard a voice. *Two voices.*

"Anyone there?" Mallon's call was met with silence, though the horses turned to look at him, wondering what he was about.

Surely Withers wasn't hiding up there! Would he even be able to manage the ladder? The man seemed hardly able to walk.

Still, Mallon was sure he'd heard something... and the only way to find out was to climb the ladder himself and take a look.

Reaching the top, he peered through the darkness.

Indeed, he'd been right. There was someone. Looking back at him was Withers—his expression filled with fear—and, next to him, another Withers, except the second looked as if he'd been to the devil and back, so gaunt and ghastly was he.

"Silas?" Mallon felt his stomach drop. Had he been here all this time? *Dear Lord, the man looked fit to drop.*

"Withers, come along now," Mallon called through the gloom. "It's going to be fine. I'm going to help."

The second face leaned forward and its owner began crawling toward the light. His voice was rougher around the edges than that of his brother, in the way a man's voice might become if he'd failed to use it a great deal. Hoarse, too, as if fighting past a lump in his throat. "Master Mallon?"

As Silas reached him, Mallon extended his hand. Questions would come later. For the moment, only reassurance was needed. Mallon squeezed Silas' fingers.

"I've got you," he said simply.

ALL THOUGHTS OF HUGO, and even of Geneviève, vanished as Mallon helped Withers and his brother descend from the hayloft.

It seemed incredible. *Silas was alive!* His face had been among those that had haunted Mallon through the years. He'd suffered under the cold hand of the late viscount, just as Mallon had—but with far more horrifying consequences. Mallon had been powerless to act all those years ago, but mightn't he have stirred himself to Silas's defense before now? Had it really taken his father's death to bring him home? The knowledge shamed Mallon. In too many ways, he'd taken the easy path.

He and Withers had Silas under the arms, supporting him as he staggered around the side of the house, toward the warmth of the kitchen. The sleet was coming stronger now, blowing in their faces, accompanied by an icy wind. Mallon needed to get poor Silas comfortable. Needed to assure him that he was on his side and he'd be safe now.

As the master of Wulverton Hall, it was Mallon's duty to see justice done. To speak for those who had no voice. To defend the rights of his tenants and the staff under his roof. He'd fight tooth and nail to keep Silas from going back to prison.

His duty to those living on the moor was more important than playing host to Marguerite's pompous guests. More important, even, than the pursuit of his own happiness.

As they passed the drawing room, Mallon thought of Geneviève. He'd tell her about Silas later. She'd been horrified to learn of his incarceration and his desperate escape across the moor. She'd be glad to know he was alive. Silas was in a bad way, but Mallon had confidence they'd restore him to health. With people who cared rallying to his aid, he'd surely draw upon the will to live.

Mallon looked through the French doors, wondering if Geneviève were still with Hugo or if all was now settled.

What he witnessed sent ice about his heart.

Geneviève was holding Hugo's hand.

Hugo was holding a ring.

And then they were holding each other.

The last thing he saw was the two of them exchanging a kiss.

CHAPTER TWENTY-FIVE

MRS. FUDDLEBY WAS CARVING thick slices of pork (from a joint Mallon suspected was destined for Upstairs luncheon) "I'm glad to be putting food on a proper plate for ye at last, Silas! 'Stead o' wrapping up scraps in a cloth for Withers to take out to ye!" She glanced over at Mallon. "An' I know the Master won't be taking umbrage, seein' as ye be one of us!"

Withers's eyes darted to Mallon and then to his brother. Wrapped under several blankets and with his chair pulled close to the stove, Silas was sipping from a steaming cup.

"Him started to take bad, and with the weather be turnin', I'd no choice but t'bring he into proper shelter. I wanted to tell ee, Master, but I feared as to what action ye'd take—Silas bein' a wanted criminal an' all, though us'uns all know he be innocent!" Withers declared.

Leaning against the edge of the great oak table, Mallon nodded. He was trying to keep his mind on what Withers was telling him, but his thoughts continued to pull toward what he'd seen through the drawing room window—Hugo proposing to Geneviève and her seeming to accept.

He couldn't deny what his own eyes had witnessed, even though his heart wanted to.

He made himself redirect his mind. Withers was trying to explain all that had happened, and he deserved Mallon's full attention.

"I'd suggested us'uns smuggled Silas to Plymouth, findin' passage on some ship. But him was too weary to attempt such a journey." Withers raised a shaking hand to take a sip from his own cup of tea.

Installed in the warmth of the kitchen, Silas seemed to have recovered some of his spirit; his voice, though still rasping, was coming back to him.

"I jus' wanted to see ye, brother! An' the hall, again. Afore I were locked up, I lived 'ere man and boy. Where else would I go?" He pressed his sleeve to his face, mumbling to himself as he wiped away the evidence of his emotion. "Only home I've ever 'ad."

Looking into the man's sunken eyes, Mallon was reminded that he'd returned to Wulverton not merely to satisfy his desire to see the moor again—no matter how burning that desire. He was here to fulfil his duty: the estate needed guidance from one who cared deeply about the well-being of its tenants; he'd felt compelled to pay his respects at his brother's grave—and those of his parents. Moreover, Silas deserved freedom from his unjust incarceration and the clearance of his name from all stain of guilt.

Those duties were Mallon's, and no one else's.

With Silas under his roof, Mallon hoped it would make the process of his release easier, rather than more complicated. As soon as possible, he'd attend upon the magistrate to petition for Silas's pardon. He had faith justice would be served.

"You're my responsibility now, Silas. No one shall send you back. Whatever years are left to you, they'll be spent here, with us."

Silas sniffed and sat as upright as he was able. "God bless ee, Master! I trust ee to speak fer me."

Withers nodded his thanks to Mallon, then closed his eyes and leant back in his chair. The strain of keeping his brother safely hidden had taken its toll. Withers looked as if he needed a week in bed himself.

Mrs. Fuddleby paused in her slathering of butter on a thick slice of bread, appearing to wipe away a tear of her own. "It's time this'un injustice be put right, and if anyone can do it, it be our master."

Mallon knew full well that Silas's incarceration had been a travesty—the result of his own father's misguided wrath on discovering his wife's infidelity. Poor Silas had only done as his mistress had asked, providing her with a horse on the night of her escape.

It seemed Silas had known her intent, but how could he have foreseen the mare would carry Mallon's mother to her death in the mire, or that the late viscount would punish him so unjustly for having done her bidding.

Only once had Mallon dared broach the subject with his father. As a child, he'd understood only that the stableman who'd taught him to ride had gone away. Reaching manhood, he'd learned the full story and had been horrified. His father had stolen a man's liberty—his life!

The accusation of 'horse theft' should never have stood up in court, but the late viscount had bribed the magistrate to pronounce the harsh sentence.

Mallon could hardly credit that Silas was still alive after all those nights hiding on the moor. He'd spent the first in a *kistvaen*, huddled in the ancient hollow of some other man's burial, hoping he'd see the sunrise without freezing to death. After that, he'd made toward the hall, knowing his brother would help him. Taking shelter in the chapel had hardly been better than exposure on the moor, since the place had no form of heating and was as cold as any grave. It had been Withers's idea to bring Silas into the hayloft above the stables.

Withers had taken Scroggins into his confidence, as well as Mrs. Fuddleby. Between them, they'd done what they'd thought best.

As Mallon rose, Withers also pushed himself to his feet.

"There be another matter, Master, if you can spare the time t'hear me."

Withers was not a man to ask favors, nor to gossip.

"Of course." Mallon offered his arm. "We'll withdraw to your butler's parlor, shall we? I've already sent Ida to make sure the fire is lit. I want you to rest for the next few days. The first footman can take some of your duties, until you're feeling stronger."

Withers nodded mutely, allowing himself to be led. His little parlor was just big enough to hold the table at which Withers sat to record his accounts of the wine and spirits used in the house. There was a single, battered armchair, too, in the corner, beside a small fire grate. Withers folded himself into it, while Mallon took the harder seat.

The butler passed his hand over his forehead before speaking, clearly anxious, but needing to relieve his conscience of some burden.

"Come, Withers, you can tell me." Mallon leant forward upon his knees.

"I be ashamed, m'Lord, seein' as it caused trouble to the lady, but 'tis best you know, and p'raps ye may set her mind to rest."

Mallon had no idea what Withers was talking about, but gave his encouragement nonetheless.

"'Tis the dogs, y'see. That Sergeant Hawky what came when Silas first made escape, with them other poor sods, him was sayin' they'd be scourin' the moor until all was recaptured."

Withers grimaced. "I were that worried, thinkin' the police'd be sniffin' round, or some other folk who'd pass on a sightin'—in hope of a reward, as it were. They might've found Silas up at the chapel, so I made sure Master Hugo's dogs were gettin' short rations, to keep 'em a bit 'ungry like, then let 'em out around dusk each night, to prowl an' scare off anyone close by."

He took out a handkerchief to blow his nose. "I were hopin' folks would think the Wisht Hounds were about, and word would travel to stop 'em wantin' to venture near."

Withers shook his head and seemed to shrink in his chair. "Wicked o' me I know! Not that the dogs will've suffered much. They'ums are always snaffling bits o' food orf the floors! But I felt bad about the lady, when her did come over in that faint, seein' our shaggy beasts up by the chapel. Mrs. Fuddleby told I about it, an' I knew straight orf it were Master Hugo's daft buggers that did it. More like to lick a man to death than anythin' else, but us'uns know what it be like after dark on the moor. Yer imagination can make ye think all sorts."

"You did right to tell me," said Mallon. "Though I wouldn't worry unduly about the countess. She's made of sterner stuff than she appears."

Withers picked up the poker and gave the logs a push before looking back to Mallon. Despite having admitted his folly, his face remained downcast.

"There's summat else, m'lord, that's been playin' terrible on my mind since Silas did tell me." He gave a shiver. "It be about Master Hugo's guest, as came in the fancy motor car."

Mallon frowned. That swine Slagsby had disappeared the day of the hunt, and Mallon had been glad of it, even though it had distressed Hugo. It had been 'good riddance' as far as Mallon was concerned.

Withers seemed to steel himself to say what he next needed to. "The young man set orf just afore the mist came down. You remember, m'lord, it were quite bad by around midday."

Mallon nodded. An uneasy feeling twisted his gut—a feeling he knew what Withers was going to tell him.

"Silas says he were driving like a madman. From up on the hill, above the chapel, he watched him headin' orf, but not in the direction o' the main road. Somehow, he took the track toward Fox Tor. He'un must've realized his mistake, for he did fix himself about, but then he took the wrong turn altogether—down the old track that goes toward the mire."

Withers' face had become bloodless, his hands shaking in his lap.

"The mist had started rollin' over by then, and Silas do say him can't be sure, but he heard a shout, way off, and then, when the next wave of mist had passed over, the car was nowhere to be seen—as if the devil had swallowed it whole."

Mallon's stomach lurched. Beware the mire, so every moorlander said, and they were right. Its bewitching landscape held him under its spell, but it was a treacherous lover to those who entered its embrace unwary.

He'd have happily given Slagsby more than a bloody nose the night he'd attacked Geneviève. He'd cursed him to hell as Hugo had escorted him back to his bed, but he would never have wished him to such an end as this—dragged to a slow, terrifying death in the mire!

Mallon's head swam at the imagining of it. The mire near Fox Tor. The same mire in which his mother had probably met her end. He clutched at the armrests on his chair, suddenly desperate for a glass of whisky to steady his nerves.

Withers was speaking again, obliging Mallon to push aside those grim images, drawing him back to the here and now.

"I sent Scroggins to look all along that'n road. He found the lord's scarf twisted upon a bush at the edge o' the bog, like as if he'd gotten hisself out o' the sinkin' car and was a-tryin' to pull hisself to safety."

Withers shook his head. "No good o' course. It ne'er be any good."

With a shudder, he hid his face in his hands. "May God forgive us, we kept it t'ourselves—just until Silas be gotten away, like. But the gennleman'll have family what'll be worryin'—and Master Hugo should know."

A creeping cold rose through Mallon's body. He'd report the death to the magistrate—better that than getting the local police involved. The telephone exchange went through Princetown. He'd be able to place a call and arrange a meeting. Only then would he tell Hugo and contact Slagsby's people. It was a nasty business, but things had to be faced head-on.

Withers raised his head again, looking Mallon straight in the eyes, making sure he was listening.

"No matter the sins upon our heads, there always be those that do love us."

CHAPTER TWENTY-SIX

WHAT A RELIEF IT HAD BEEN! Geneviève had dreaded Hugo pleading with her to change her mind or—worse still—a torrent of tears. *Ha!* How conceited to believe she'd inspired such devotion! He'd diverted his attention to Beatrice with mercurial speed.

Geneviève couldn't help but congratulate herself on ensuring Hugo suffered no heartbreak, but also on the decision she'd made. Impossible, now, to think she could ever have been content as Hugo's wife.

She'd thought a malleable husband to be just what she needed—one whose mind she could shape to her own ends. How very foolish she'd been. Only on meeting Mallon had she realized her desire for union with one she could both admire and respect. Far better to be equals in intellect and to treat one another as such. She was willing, even, to concede Mallon's superiority in some matters (alongside her own in others, of course).

Giving Hugo the jewels had been the right thing to

do. If she were to commit to a life with Mallon, she needed to set aside the past, and that included the Rosseline diamonds.

Maxim had given them to her on their wedding day, his fingers—always so cool and elegant—fastening them about her neck and wrist. She'd never dreamed of owning such jewels. Knowing they were hers had been exhilarating. The diamonds had proclaimed her elevation. She'd arrived at last!

He'd clipped the large pendants to her ears, then kissed the length of her throat, whispering how beautiful she looked.

Later, she recalled, he'd removed all her clothing and taken his pleasure of her body, adorned in nothing but those diamonds. She remembered every time she wore them. Every time she looked at them.

Maxim had given her so much, but not love. Never love.

The diamonds represented all she'd clung to. All she'd aspired to. Château Rosseline would always hold warm memories for her, but her heart no longer hungered to call it home, for she'd found something more captivating. As for the approval of those noble families she'd once yearned to emulate—she cared not a jot!

She had Mallon now, and he was real. His feelings for her were real. They would be everything to one another. One day, perhaps, there would be a child. Warmth blossomed through her, and she rested a hand on the curve of her belly, a smile touching her lips.

Married to the man she admired and loved, safe in

his arms, building a life together on this mysterious, dangerous, bewitching moor. And a baby for them to love, together.

Geneviève wanted all of it, forever, and she wanted forever to start right away.

MALLON NEEDED to speak to Geneviève, and as soon as possible. He knew he must allow her to explain. He owed her that.

He looked for her in the drawing room, in the library, and then the salon before realizing that, within the hour, Marguerite wished them to assemble for carol singing about the great tree in the hall. Geneviève had probably gone to change her dress.

Though he walked briskly up the stairs, by the time he reached the corridor to her bedroom, his feet were lagging. Standing before her door, he almost feared to knock.

When he did so, she opened it immediately, bidding him inside. She wore the dress of red silk he so admired, though not her ostentatious jewels. Her earrings, tonight, were simple jet, her throat bare of adornment.

He opened his mouth to speak, but she flung her arms about his neck, pulling him down to meet her kiss, folding her body to him. He wrapped his arms about her waist and squeezed her tightly.

The kiss endured for some minutes before he had the will to break away. It was a kiss sweeter than any she'd given him—a kiss of tenderness and longing, leisurely and insistent. The sort of kiss a bride would give to her groom, knowing they had a lifetime, and more than a thousand kisses yet to come.

She was so beautiful. She always would be. Even in another forty years, the same bright light would flash from those stormy, violet eyes, and her lips would beckon as they did now.

But he wouldn't be the man to see those enchantments.

She must have sensed something was wrong, for her eyebrows knitted. She raised her hand to touch his cheek, and he took it in his, turning it to kiss her palm, then her fingers. He gave it back to her then, and a little crease formed above her nose.

His throat felt constricted, but he forced a cough and said, "You've settled everything with Hugo?" His voice sounded strange, as if from far away.

"Yes! All done." She took his hand in both of hers and raised it to her lips, kissing his fingers as he'd done to her.

"And your decision, Geneviève?" He forced himself to look at her, needing to hear her say the words.

"My decision?" She looked genuinely puzzled. "Haven't you and I already made that together?"

He hated to tell her that he'd spied upon them, although it hadn't quite been like that. It had been sheer happenstance that he'd glanced them through the window.

"I saw you, Geneviève, with Hugo. I saw him offer you the ring. Did you accept?" The last word seemed to exit his mouth more sharply than the rest, with its own keen edge.

"No! You're quite wrong." She gave a faltering laugh. "Hugo wasn't giving the ring to me; it was I who presented it to him!" She shook her head. "I mean, the ring belonged to Hugo's grandmother. I've given it to him."

"Very generous of you." Mallon was aware his voice had become a deadened monotone. His face felt rigid.

"Mallon?" Geneviève blinked and frowned. "I don't understand. Has something changed?"

He sighed, and it felt like the last breath of a dying man. An ache had begun beneath his ribs, knowing what he intended to say.

They'd promised to have no secrets, in those long hours in which they'd laid in each other's arms. After a lifetime of hurt and resentment, he'd wanted to let those feelings go. He'd wanted to believe in her, and in himself. He wanted to clutch at the knowledge she was his, and always would be.

Perhaps she was telling him the truth. There was something in her expression that made him believe so, but he realized it didn't matter if he'd been mistaken in what he'd seen.

Her promises of fidelity wouldn't be enough. She could tell him a hundred times he was her only love and it would make no difference. For the seed of doubt had been sown, and it had made him realize he'd never be free of his uncertainty. What sort of future would they have if he couldn't bring himself to believe in the trust she placed in him?

She might stand before the altar and pledge herself to him but, in his heart of hearts, he would be waiting for the day when all would come crashing down. Could he put himself through loving her with his entire soul and then endure the agony of losing her love?

If she disappointed him, how could he live with that failure and pain, as his father had done? Loving and trusting her and then losing it all would render him a shadow of himself.

"I can't," he said simply. "I thought I could, and I wanted to, and no other woman has made me feel that I might…"

Dear God, he sounded like Hugo. For a moment, he thought he might laugh, but he found the eruption in his throat wasn't laughter but a choked-back sob, and his eyes were prickling.

"Mallon!" Geneviève shouted after him as he strode away, but he didn't look back.

CHAPTER TWENTY-SEVEN

THERE HAD BEEN times in his childhood when Mallon had wished he wasn't a human boy at all. How much simpler to be a hare on the moor—running wild and answerable to no one, and with a deep burrow to escape into. He wanted to be the hare now—to retreat and lock the door, and bury himself where none could see him.

He feared if he did so, he'd never come out.

Instead, he put on his evening attire and brushed his hair. He would go down and behave as if everything were fine. No one needed to know his world had shrunk to nothingness. Pain was always worst at the beginning. He just needed some months and he might be able to think of this night with some equanimity.

He descended the stairs as late as possible, receiving a flash of annoyance from Marguerite. Scanning the heads of those below, he saw Geneviève was absent. That was a relief, at least. Had she been there, his resolution might have been dashed, and he'd have fallen back into the pit he so feared—that place in which he was powerless to stop someone he cared about from hurting him.

Mallon moved among his guests, shaking hands. Finding Reverend Wapshot, he thanked him for having offered to lead them in a Christmas service later, just before midnight. Mallon accepted a cinnamon biscuit but his mouth was dry. He broke off a small piece and it seemed to stick in his throat. From a passing tray, he accepted a glass of mulled wine, when what he really wanted was an entire bottle of whisky.

He thought, momentarily, of escaping to the kitchen and hiding down there with Mrs. Fuddleby, but that was a ridiculous notion.

Alongside everyone else, he clapped at the lighting of the Yule Log. Scroggins had been tasked with finding a large chunk of oak—a piece sizeable enough to burn right through until midnight chimed, when they'd all greet one another with joyful Christmas tidings in the chapel. It had been many years since Mallon had participated in the custom, but he remembered how it had made him feel as a boy—wistful and expectant.

Once, dreams of the future had been hopeful, despite the pain of his mother's absence. The Eve of Christmas had been magical, as those dark hours passed in awaiting the coming of the Savior. Of course, many of the Christian rituals were mere adaptations of their pagan predecessors. Nevertheless, he remembered the excitement he'd felt. Tonight, there was no room in his heart for joy.

Marguerite summoned their attention and announced the singing of their first carol, a French setting of *Away in a Manger*. Beatrice, of course, had been asked to accompany them on the piano, which had been rolled into the hall. The melody was heartbreakingly familiar, and Mallon found himself listening to the voices around him, seeking out one that would be lovelier than the rest. Geneviève would have a beautiful singing voice, he felt sure, though he'd never heard her sing. She'd chosen to be the hare, and he couldn't blame her.

The next was *O Holy Night*, and the words were so tender and hopeful he felt his throat again constricting, a piercing ache building in his heart.

He hadn't explained his fears very well to Geneviève, that was for sure.

Mallon's thoughts drifted back to Constantinople, where he'd sought out the Holy Spirit Cathedral for midnight mass. Whatever darkness filled a man's soul, there was comfort in the thought of a higher power. Comfort in the notion of the divine—of man being loved unconditionally by his maker. Comfort, too, in the thought of humanity linking arms in goodwill.

He wanted to believe in man's ability for goodness, and his own, come to that. He wanted to put the cheerless days behind him and welcome the light of hope and joy.

But what hope could there be without Geneviève?

He remembered the day he'd driven her onto the moor. It had been cold and damp but she'd hadn't uttered one word of complaint. He'd rambled on, telling anecdotes of his childhood upon the heathland, exploring its ancient sites of standing stones and its windswept tors. She'd asked eagerly about the country-side and its history, and it had been a pleasure to share with her his love for the land.

At the inn, too, he'd felt the same desire to take her into his confidence—to reveal how it had been for him all those years ago, after his mother died.

And how right it had felt to hold her in his arms as they'd danced. His greatest moments of happiness had been those spent alone with her—and not just in the heat of passion.

The realization of his foolishness came upon him in a great surging rush. He'd wanted to believe in her love for him. To believe all the astonishing and extraordinary things she'd said to him. He'd wanted to believe he was worthy of the love she'd professed, but his self-doubt had held him back—that old fear of being betrayed and having his heart torn apart. Of being abandoned by the one who should love him best.

It had been easier to hide behind that fear than to face it down, and he'd let her go because of it! What sort of man was he? A damn foolish one, who'd rejected the woman he loved with his entire heart. It was himself he needed to trust and in the sweetness of the love she offered.

Little wonder she'd kept to her room. He'd been so afraid of having his heart broken, he'd barely consid-ered Geneviève's feelings. Was she, at that very moment, shedding tears for him? Or raging at him for not listening to her? How he must have wounded her! He'd make sure she was never hurt again, that her eyes would never look at him with such anguish. He wanted to lay the world at her feet.

He must waste no time. He must go to her and make everything right, if it was still possible. Heaven help him if he'd destroyed his chance of happiness with her.

Without waiting for the carol to end, Mallon slipped through the throng and skirted behind, toward the staircase. He needed to speak to Geneviève right away.

However, just as he was laying his hand upon the bannister, someone touched his arm. Turning, he saw it was Hugo, beaming even more effusively than usual.

"Uncle, I must share my news with you." Tugging at Mallon's sleeve, he indicated for them to retreat to the corner.

Mallon glanced up the stairs, impatient to go to Geneviève. He felt a swell of irritation, then quickly reproached himself. His nephew was cheerful by nature, but never had Mallon seen him so elated, nor so insistent to impart a message. Mallon hadn't forgotten he had news to impart—of Slagsby's death—but that could wait until Christmas had passed, at least.

Hugo's eyes were shining. "I hope it will meet with your approval. I really think it will, but your good opinion matters to me, and I want you to be the first to know, although not quite the first, perhaps, since it was the countess who made me see." His words were tumbling so fast he was making no sense at all.

"A bit slower, Hugo," Mallon urged. "Or start again, if you like, but try to be succinct."

Hugo took a deep breath and resumed. "Aunt

Geneviève told me Beatrice was holding a torch for me. Naturally, I'd not had the least notion, but I jumped in the car and went straight over. I did everything just as a man should—asked her father first, then got down on one knee and presented the ring. She said 'yes', and has made me the happiest of men."

"I don't think I even knew what true happiness was until this moment—and it's all because of Aunt Geneviève!"

Mallon was finding it all rather difficult to take in. "And the ring…" He remembered what Geneviève had told him.

"Exactly!" Hugo grinned. "All my aunt's doing! And not just the ring, either. She's given me the Rosseline diamonds in their entirety. They were hers to keep, for her lifetime, you know, but she was adamant. Something about turning a new page and having faith in the future."

Hugo rubbed his chin. "She even mentioned signing over some portion of her income from the vineyards, but I told her the estate has enough money for me to manage, and she'll need something to live upon."

Mallon was dumbstruck. Her generosity stunned him, yet it felt true to the woman he'd grown to love. She was risking her financial independence. If she did as she proposed, what safeguard would there be for her future?

Like a lightning bolt, the truth struck him. She'd believed so wholly in his steadfastness and loyalty that she'd been willing to surrender herself to his protection. Rosseline was part of her past, not her future, and her marriage to the count had been inspired not by love but by gain. In renouncing her wealth, she was demonstrating her faith in a new life with him.

Mallon felt sick with shame. He'd behaved like an ass because of his fear of Geneviève abandoning him. It hadn't been she who'd let him down. Instead, he'd deserted her.

Hugo was looking about the room. "Where is she, Uncle? I really must thank her again for her wise advice, and I know Beatrice wishes to thank her, too."

Whatever else Hugo said, Mallon never heard, for he was already taking the stairs, not caring whom among their guests thought him rude.

A Staffordshire ceramic sheep, a Donyatt jug filled with dried heather, and a matching pair of china cockerels almost went flying from a sideboard as Mallon raced down the corridor to Geneviève's room.

He didn't bother to knock. Breathless, he flung open the door.

And his heart fell to his stomach.

Several items had been left scattered about the room but, for the most part, it had been cleared. Her perfume and hairbrush were no longer on the dressing table. The wardrobe door swung ajar, revealing an empty interior.

She was gone.

CHAPTER TWENTY-EIGHT

GENEVIÈVE TOOK a last look back at the hall as the coach reached the top of the avenue, making the turn upon the road which led to Two Bridges and The Saracen's Head. Had so little time really passed since she'd first entered these gates?

In these past days, she'd come to know the only man with whom she'd thought she might have a truly happy and contented life. He wasn't like any man she'd known before. Despite a past that might have embittered him, he remained generous-hearted and honorable. As master of these lands, he offered neither condescension nor arrogance, but sympathy and protection. She admired him more than she could say, and wanted him —wanted to become part of the world she'd glimpsed through his eyes.

She'd offered him all her faith and hope, and it hadn't been enough. When Mallon had walked away, she'd felt something crack deep inside.

She wiped away a welling tear. No matter that her

heart was breaking, she wouldn't cry as she had over her mother. Better to have no heart. Better never to show her true self to anyone again.

What use was there to think of it? He'd made himself clear, even while stumbling to choose the words. He mistrusted her, or love, or both. He believed she would betray him. Perhaps not straight away, but eventually, and he wasn't prepared to risk his heart. He wanted everything to be safe! As if love could ever be that.

Not that she was an expert, but all things precious were worth fighting for, were they not?

She told herself to stop. The affair was at an end and that was that.

It had begun to snow—thick, fat flakes falling steadily, quickly dusting the heathland in a layer of white. The tops of the hills were already covered. Quite beautiful, though it would make her onward journey difficult on the morrow.

Despite being Christmas day, she'd been assured there would be a coach she might join. As to where she'd sleep, she hoped the inn would have a room. She and Lisette could share if necessary.

Where she'd go, she wasn't sure, but needed a new beginning. It just wouldn't be here, on the moor, with the man she'd come to feel so deeply for.

SCROGGINS WAS DRIVING the countess himself, the stable lad told Mallon, taking her as far as The Saracen's Head. Mallon thought of several things he'd have liked to have said about that, but bit them back. He wasn't his father, taking out his temper on those who were blameless.

And there was still time to catch them on the road. They'd been gone not half an hour and it took but a few minutes to saddle his stallion.

Riding out, he was thankful for the moon, although its illumination was dimmed significantly by the clouds rolling over the land. How long had it been snowing? Long enough to already be covering the wheel tracks from the carriage ahead.

Mallon had thrown his heaviest coat over his shoulders but, in his haste, had ignored the need for hat or gloves. He gritted his teeth against the snow blowing into his face and the biting cold on his fingers. All that mattered was having the chance to tell her what a huge fool he'd been and to beg her forgiveness.

He urged his horse up the hill, clearing the summit. From there, he could see some distance. Princetown, far off, and the prison, closer. There wasn't time to linger, but Mallon sent a silent prayer for those men incarcerated there tonight. He wished some small light of hope might penetrate their bleak lives. One, at least, would be spared another day within those walls. That was something to think of later, however. Silas had been put to bed in one of rooms usually reserved for visiting servants. He'd be safe there, and have time to recover his strength.

Mallon scanned further down the road, and his heart leapt. He saw the carriage. Giving his horse a swift kick, he galloped down the hill, hoping the stallion's footing would remain sure.

"Scroggins!" Mallon called as he drew closer. "Stop, I say!" His voice was swallowed by the whirling snow on his first shout, but the second did it, and the carriage pulled to a halt.

Someone else had heard him, too, for the carriage window was drawn down and a head appeared, looking back at him.

As he brought himself alongside, he saw her nose was pink and her eyes a little bleary, but she had never looked more beautiful to him.

He hadn't known what to expect. Tears perhaps. Instead, she was looking at him in just the way he'd hoped, her eyes full of tenderness. Those eyes striated silver through deepest violet! He felt a rush of wonder, tumbling headlong into her gaze, and reached for her, wanting to touch her hand at least.

However, she suddenly turned to sneeze, fumbling with a handkerchief, and when she looked back, she appeared rather cross.

"You came to find me, though you've told me more than once that it would be better for me to leave Wulverton. You've won, at last. I'm going, and there's no reason for me to return."

The stallion tossed its head, unhappy about being kept standing in the snow. Mallon was obliged to tug on the bridle to keep the mount from skittering. "Hear me out, Geneviève."

"You think I have no feelings...but it hurts to see you, and I'd rather not be hurt." She was biting at her lip, reluctant to look at him now.

He reached for the edge of the window and located

her hand, clasping his fingers through hers. At her touch, a terrible ache lurched inside him, as if his heart would burst and break. He needed to convince her, though he hardly knew where to begin.

She tugged her hand away. "If you think so little of me, what more can there be to say? You care for me, I know, yet you won't fight for us. Instead, you run away." She closed her eyes and swallowed hard, clearly holding back tears.

"I've been a fool." Blurting it seemed the best way. Mallon knew he had to tell her everything. If he didn't now, when would there ever be the time? "I was a coward and an imbecile, but I've realized what you mean to me, Geneviève. I was living a half-life, pretending that I didn't need anyone, refusing to allow myself to love, for fear of being disappointed."

She was listening, but she still looked forlorn. "I want to believe you, Mallon, but I'm not sure I can make things right. I've tried…"

He could tell she was trying to keep her voice from trembling. A tear rolled down her cheek.

"I need you." He drew closer, reaching to touch where the teardrop was descending. "Forgive me for hurting you. Forgive me for being so damn blinded." He spoke softly yet with urgency and sincerity. "Forgive me Geneviève, and love me, just as I love you."

It was the first time that he'd said it and he was shocked to hear the words. He'd thought they would be so hard to say, but they'd flown out just when he'd required them. Why had it been so hard for him to admit before?

She jerked, then faltered into absolute stillness. Her lips parted, her beautiful eyes wide, looking back at him. "You love me?" She raised her hand to wipe away the wetness on her cheek.

"Of course, I do. And I want you to belong to me. I love you and I never want to let you go."

He meant every word. From this day forward, he'd never let a day go by without ensuring she felt adored.

"Never?" She sniffed again, but managed a smile.

"I want to hold you and kiss you. For us to be together always. If you'll let me, I'll adore you, with all my heart and body. I'll have Reverend Wapshot read the banns at the next Sunday mass. I've been waiting quite long enough for my life to begin. Now I've found you, I don't want to waste a single day, not an hour, even."

Leaning out of the carriage window, Geneviève threw her arms about his neck, pulling him to her kiss. In it he tasted forgiveness, love, and a promise of what might be, of the future they might forge together. When she broke off, it was to gather her skirts. She pushed open the door and stepped down, onto the crunch of snow.

"You've room for another in your saddle, I suppose?" As she looked up at Mallon, he felt that his heart had been aching for this since their first encounter, though he hadn't known, then, what those feelings had meant.

He quickly dismounted and helped her climb up, to sit in front of him, pulling her into his warmth, just as on the day she'd been thrown in the mire.

"You might have stayed warm in the carriage, you

know," said Mallon, brushing her ear and her neck with his lips.

"Except the carriage is going the wrong way, taking Lisette back to the hall." Geneviève twisted to look at him, with mischief in her eyes. "If you want our lives together to begin right now, I suggest we ride to The Saracen's Head, and see if they have a room."

"A scandalous idea!" Mallon's lips twitched in suppressed laughter.

"Might your reputation stand it?" teased Geneviève. "We can book two rooms if you like, but I shall expect to have the better of them, and you must do the creeping along the corridor."

He kissed her before she could say another word. He was no longer afraid. He would love her with his body and his heart, and risk whatever followed.

"I love you." Geneviève spoke the words softly, but they came to rest in Mallon's soul. He believed her.

Mallon stirred his horse into action. "Quite right, too! Now, I'm going to show you just what it means to be loved, Geneviève. Most thoroughly!"

He knew that everything would unfold with time and, having each other, it would all come right. They would wake on Christmas morning as they meant to go on, believing in the power of love to conquer all.

EPILOGUE

Wulverton Hall, 1909

"When will Daddy come up and see me? I spotted a red kite on the moor today. It's my job, he says, to keep an eye on the birds. He'll want to know about the kite."

Young Edward's head rested on his pillow and his eyes were growing heavy, but his father had been away since the previous Monday, and Edward was eager to speak to him. Lord Wulverton's returning carriage had pulled up before the hall as the boy had been changing into his night shirt.

For the past few years, Mallon had been taking more trips to London, speaking in favor of women's suffrage at the House of Lords. The concerns of the moorlanders always came first, but Viscount Wulverton had decided he couldn't remain silent on the issue of women's entitlement to an equal voice. He'd vowed to use his own in their support.

Geneviève gently stroked her son's dark curls. How

like his father he was, with his green eyes and his father's passion for the moor. Not even five years old, he already knew the names of so many of the plants and creatures that inhabited the wild lands of the Wulverton estate.

"He'll be with us very soon, to tuck you in." Geneviève placed a kiss on Edward's cheek. Having divested himself of his coat, Mallon would come straight upstairs, she knew.

Some moments later, stepping softly across the room, Lord Wulverton met his wife's lips in a kiss, before drawing up a chair on the opposite side of the bed.

"I knew you'd be back today, Daddy," murmured Edward sleepily, endeavouring to waken himself again. "And I've lots to tell you…"

"I thought of you and your mama every day, little man, and I want to hear your report on everything — but perhaps in the morning." Mallon caught Geneviève's eye as she pushed herself upright, cradling the curve of her growing stomach. Only another month or so, and there would be another child to occupy the nursery.

Don't be long, she mouthed, holding his gaze for just long enough to leave no doubt of her meaning. Quietly, she made her way down the corridor to their own bedroom.

"Tell me a story, Daddy," mumbled Edward. "The one I like best." The lad curled onto his side.

"Close your eyes again then," said Mallon, rubbing Edward's back, "And imagine a great wide sea filled with ships." He dropped his voice low as he recited the melody of the words. "Each ship carries valiant soldiers, commanded by the most courageous of them all, pledged in allegiance to their king."

Mallon began the list of noble warriors, just as his own father had told him, once upon a time. His mother had kissed him goodnight then, and his father had sat in this same chair, and Mallon had whispered the names alongside, just as Edward did now.

"De Moray of Rouen, de Reyne of Morlaix, de Winter of the House of Bourbon, de Russe of Flanders, St. Hèver of Normandy, de Lara of Boucau, Wellesbourne of Wales, du Reims of Reims, de Lohr of Lohr..."

"And de Wolfe," whispered Edward.

"And de Wolfe," repeated Mallon, "Of the House of Vargr—the kings of Breton."

"That's us, isn't it, Daddy?" Edward sighed, burying his face against the pillow.

"It is. All the way from France, just like your mama, but a long time ago." Lord Wulverton pulled the quilt up a little higher over his son's shoulders.

"And we're brave, too, aren't we, Daddy." Edward's voice was almost muffled by the covers. "I'll be like you, when I'm big and, if there's a battle, I'll be a soldier." He gave a yawn. "Or I might go to London and speak in Parliament...and tell them all to be good...or I could just stay here and look after you and Mama, and everyone on the moor."

Mallon sat for a moment, listening to the gentle breathing of the sleeping child, before turning out the lamp.

In the passageway, the moon shone through the far window, and the door of his bedchamber was ajar.

She was already under the covers when he entered, waiting for him. Her eyes, darkest amethyst, told him that she was ready. As he came close, she pulled loose his tie, then tugged to bring his mouth to hers.

He had truly found his way home.

THE 'LADY'S GUIDE' SERIES

You'll find adventure, intrigue, mystery, and romance in this witty and exciting series.
No young woman worth her salt wants to be advised by a pompous 'Lady's Guide', but this particular volume is rather unconventional.

Try as they might, our heroines can't deny that its advice sometimes comes up trumps!

Discover heroines who know their own mind, and heroes who appreciate a woman's worth.

'The Lady's Guide to a Highlander's Heart'

What dark secret does her lover hide?
Upon the night of her hasty betrothal, Flora's father is
murdered.
With eyes black as midnight, and a savage soul, her
fearsome warrior husband seems to care nothing for his
bride.
Believing him guilty of the foul deed, Flora flees the
castle.
Years later, swearing revenge, she returns in disguise.
But, she is soon consumed by conflicting desires.
Is the man she begins to care for truly her father's
murderer?

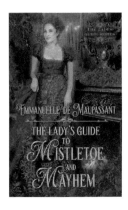

'The Lady's Guide to Mistletoe and Mayhem'

On the run from an unwanted marriage, Ursula assumes the identity of an etiquette teacher and heads to a remote Scottish castle for the Yuletide season, but her 'young charge' turns out to be more than she bargained for.
Texan rancher Rye Dalreagh, the long lost Dunrannoch heir, has been thrown in the deep end. During what should be the merriest of seasons, he must choose a bride, navigate an ancient curse, avoid being murdered, and try not to fall in love with his manners tutor.

'The Lady's Guide to Escaping Cannibals'

Under the protection of darkly handsome Captain Jorge de Silva, Lady Bathsheba Asquith lands on the mysterious island of Vanuaka with only three days to find her missing brother.

The trials of the jungle strip away any pretense of propriety and passion flares, but de Silva is not all he seems, and Bathsheba is in more danger than she can imagine.

Vanuaka's volcano is awakening—and only a human sacrifice can appease its fire.

MORE IN THE 'LADY'S GUIDE'
SERIES

Releasing through 2021 and beyond

The Lady's Guide to Scandal
The Lady's Guide to Deception and Desire
The Lady's Guide to a Sultan's Harem
The Lady's Guide to Transylvanian Terrors

A NOTE FROM EMMANUELLE

If you'd like to receive 'first eyes' on more stories, please do sign up for my mailing list, so you'll never miss a thing, and you'll also receive a *free* book from my 'Lady's Guide' series. (just visit my website to find out more - www.emmanuelledemaupassant.com)

If you're on Facebook, do hop on over to join my reader group. All sorts of 'insider info' there (mostly photos of our beloved Scotland, and our lovely new puppy Archie)

I'm there most days to chat, including sharing recommendations from my own tottering reading pile.

Everyone is welcome.

See you there.

Do you have a moment to leave a review?
(it's the best gift you can offer an author)

Find **Master of the Moor** on Goodreads, Amazon and Bookbub.

LAURA BARBER

Goddess

Poetry Collection

First edition

Dedicated to myself, because not enough things are.

Contents

Kore

Spring

Death

Persephone

Kore

The maiden

Attention

It's nice to feel wanted but,
There is something to be said,
For the thrill of the chase.

The effort I put into getting someone,
Is rendered non-grata once they meet me halfway,
And that's why I never tire of you.

Because no matter how much attention I get from every other soul,
No matter how many eyes I feel rest on the small of my back,

I only crave attention from you.

And the fact you don't want me,
Makes it so much more satisfying,
When I can fool myself into thinking you do.

Eyes

Though worn a little around the edges,
For which I must take some credit,
Your eyes, so similar, but unlike mine,
Do look on me anew,
And in them, I see what you hoped for me all along.

Lonely

There is a loneliness to being a child. One that I dread to go back to. I think of childhood and my first thought is never of games and friends and dinners with my family. My mind goes to nights alone in my room where I tell myself I am as hateful as they say and I ache for my mother but can't bear to take comfort in her because the loneliness is now my friend.

Have you ever felt that lonely? For loneliness to become your friend. To crave the sorrow of solitude and carve out a space where you can be lonely in a crowd. There is a loneliness to being a child. One I hope I never make friends with again.

Nostalgia

My mother told me not to begrudge somebody of nostalgia.
That to reminisce doesn't mean to miss someone.

And although I hated that time in my life,
I do miss who we were together sometimes.

So I won't begrudge somebody of nostalgia
And I hope that you won't begrudge it of me.

Overdrawn

I've spent my life convincing myself that a moment is enough. That I can have a glimpse of something and never speak of it again. As if I could preserve the memory under glass and visit it when I pleased. I'd polish it to stop the dust from settling. Keep it alive and gleaming. But of course, a moment is never enough. And a memory never measures up to the present, no matter how well you document it. You cannot re-feel the warmth on your skin or re-smell the scent of comfort. Eventually, the dust will gather and the colours will fade and I can no longer pay back the debt I've created. I become more overdrawn for the promise of one more moment. A promise I never keep.

The Game

Was I supposed to understand the game?
I tried to play along,
But I didn't have all the pieces,
And now I do,
I still feel like I could hand them all over to you.

Unwanted

I pretend to lose interest in friendships as soon as I see I'm not wanted. Friends aren't supposed to make you feel lonely like that, but they do. Pretending is the least painful way to be sometimes.

Why

Even now I wonder why you called me,
Whether you thought I was beautiful,
If you didn't want me,
Why did you tell me you did?
Worse, why did I believe it?

Worth

It's hard to love yourself when someone treats you like shit. But even harder when they treat you like you're worth something.

Love

I love you is not an all-access pass. It is not a free ticket to hurt me with the expectation I will still come back for more. Because I will.

Depression

I take my depression to bed with me.
Introduce it to my sheets and hold it gently while I try to sleep.

I have become a shadow again. Fading around the edges, fraying at the seams asking to be seen.

Stay with me, she says. *Stay here with me.*
OK, you reply. *I will.*
I'll stay. I'll stay. I'll stay.

Wrong

You think there's something wrong with you. Some odious oversight that leaves you feeling outside yourself and that scares you.

But if there isn't something wrong with you, that's even scarier.
If everyone feels like this then how do you deal with that?

You do selfish things to make yourself feel better. You hurt people and push them away and that's OK because it is proof. Proof there is something wrong with you. Isn't there?

Spring
The goddess

Bloom

You gave me roots and watered me,
You pruned me, sometimes harshly,
You showed your spine,
And taught me how to grow my own,
And turn my face towards the light.

You are limitless,
And now I can be too.

For now, I am ready,
I am ready for it all,
For the sun, the moon and stars,
I am in bloom.

First

I hope you're your first.
I hope you are your first.

Your first friend,
Your first love,
Your first home,
Your first solace,

Your first experience of kindness,
Your first passion,
Your first fight,
Your first middle of the night,

Your first lover,
Your first reason to be,
Your first everything.

I hope you are your first.

Cry

Tears for me are an infrequent thing,
Usually reserved for frustration and funerals,
My very own death and taxes.

Most people brag about this,
How it takes so much to burst the dam,
That the last time they felt their pain on their cheeks was when
they were a child.

It is apparently a strength to be unfeeling,
Which is strange because the strongest people I know,
Are the most affected by theirs.

And then there is me,
Not a cold unfeeling thing but still,
Hidden behind a window that only comprehends anger and
delight.

And it is times like these that I wonder if I should cry more.
Because I worry that I will not grow,
Without my fair share of rain.

A Mother's Love

I'm sad. So utterly sad that I have to teach you to be afraid. That
I have to teach you
not to trust the world and hold yourself back.
That you will be hurt and I might not be able to stop it.
I'm sad that I'm raising you to be a human when there are
others out there

who aren't teaching their boys the same. Who are teaching
boys to take from you, that it doesn't matter if they destroy you.

Because you are worth far more than what they want from you.

And I now understand why Demeter went to such great lengths
to shield her daughter. And how she almost starved the world
when she was taken. Because a world that uses you up doesn't
deserve my love.

When You Look At Me

And when you look at me,
With those fresh eyes, those eyes that haven't even decided
on their hue,
Those eyes that haven't even decided how they will end up
just yet,

I see the measure of what you are and how nothing will ever be
more important than you.

Favourite

You were, by no means my first love and
You are, of course, not my only,
But you will always be my greatest love and most definitely,
My favourite.

Cuckoo

When I was younger, people seldom saw me as my mother's daughter.

Especially when my sisters were with us, their fair skin and matching features only accentuated the contrasting tones that set me apart. I always felt like the cuckoo of the family, a stranger in its adoptive nest. Only when my dad was around, did I seem to fit, as his presence seemed to put me into context just on the basis of the colour of our skin.

And now I am grown and I see my mother in me. In the shape of our words, the curve of our mouths and the interests we share. But now I am the mother and I am searching for the similarities I share with you.

I lament that you don't look like me. That where my skin is warm and brown yours is light and pink. It's hard for me that people don't automatically know that we belong together. Maybe especially so, as you have the same complexion as my own mother. You have my sister's shared face and Goddess only knows who's green eyes.

And somehow.

Somehow, even though I birthed you from my own body, made every detail of your embodied self with my own, you are still so different to me.

I'm glad you look like you but I can't help but feel,
Sometimes,
That I am still the cuckoo.

I Love You

I love you. A lot. As much as I can.
And that is poetry enough for me.

Jabs

You got your jabs during a heatwave.
So we spent the afternoon eating ice cream in bed,
With the curtains drawn and flapping in the breeze of the fan
rotating by our feet.

And I realised no one had ever needed me as much, no one had
just needed me to exist, like You do right now face stuck to my
chest softly snoring near my ear.

And one day this feeling,
This need will be gone.
You will be off doing your own thing,
And the thought of a hug will make you want to pull your arms
off.
But right now I will count every kiss,
And savour every cuddle,
And smile every time you stroke my arms affectionately.

I will love you just for existing, just like you love me right now
because I do.

Men

Never did I question where I learned to be gentle of rejecting men. I am always not to bruise their feelings at the expense of my own.

no thanks means no. I'm fine means no. an awkward laugh means no. silence means no.

I hope one day our daughters will travel safely by moonlight, giving thanks for her watchful gaze. Assured that no man can hurt her because his manhood entitles him to do so.

Seeds

You sewed a field of seeds beneath my skin,
Seeds of love, seeds of doubt,
A wildflower mix of all we could be

Like a garden,
Full of weeds, you wrangle around my limbs,
And hold me still

You creep around my lungs,
And even though, you envelop me in darkness, I
know nothing else

Your grip suffocates like a warm embrace,
The thorns pierce my soul in sadistic release,
And I almost crave the pain

It is for this reason,
I was always caught between watering the seeds,
On cultivating these weeds,

Or digging them up,
With my bare hands,

And creating a garden of my own.

You

My mother always tells me that I will one day regret the ink on my skin

And I always reply that I never could.

I've reasoned with myself, that even when they no longer look as they once did
Even when they fold and ripple until they're more abstract than art
Even if I decide I no longer like birds or flowers or the female form
They will always be a memory of a past self at different points in time.

But I may have been a bit hasty,
A tad pre-emptive,
A touch presumptuous,
When I carved the words into my skin that declare that

I belong deeply to myself

Because I didn't realise it was a lie.
Because I, of course, now know, I will always, belong deeply to

You

Death

The Queen

I Want More Romance in My Friendships

Is it OK to be a little bit in love with your friends? To want to climb all over them, to hold their hand and rest your head in their lap. Have them touch your face and stroke your hair. Kiss you gently on the lips and tangle their legs around yours. Tell each other you love the other whenever there is a gap in conversation. Not to fill the silence, but just to reaffirm it. Can you do all of this without it meaning anything more than what it is? Just a kindness between friends. I want more romance in my friendships.

Breaths

My demons live in the breaths you take between words. Ready to claw my lungs out any chance they get. One day they might devour me whole.

What's in a Name?

I never identified with my name either.
I was fortunate not to be called "little girl" but it has never fit
me all the same.

I even hated it in my younger years, my skin would buzz and
my heart would ache when those I love called me by my name.
I'll admit
I have, in recent years tried to claim it.
To offer it out to those I meet but if you were to speak my name
when it was only me and you
to tell me that I was the one to make you come undone,
I'd think you're talking to someone else.
Because inside I'm am Persephone not Kore.
The bringer of chaos not some hapless maiden.

Not anymore.

Hardship

I deal in desires you can never fulfil. The desire for passion and pain

aren't they the same?

I mistake the easiness of our love for lack. If it isn't hard it isn't love. And that's not to say it isn't hard. Because it is. But it's a much more palatable hard than my ideas of it. It's not the hardship of loneliness or fear or the anticipation of abandonment. In fact I take for granted that it never crosses my mind (only maybe sometimes in my dreams) that we would ever lead lives away from each other.

I think our hardships are more about the repetition and routine. The same argument we had last month, the "why did you spend money on that", or "you didn't listen to me". The times we sit next to each other and don't speak because we're both too exhausted and the energy to give context is too much.

But sometimes I think the black and white turbulence is easier to understand. And maybe my desire for something more clear cut is wasted. Maybe I'm ungrateful for the harmony we've created because when everything is quiet, I think I want a little more passion and pain in our hardship.

Skin

How funny that my skin is such a comfort to you, the pulled
warm thickness of it,
I watch you pluck at my collar bone as if it was your instrument
to play.
As far as you're concerned it is,
You pull at my throat, trying to shift the pips that have become
lodged there,
As if asking me why I chose to swallow them in the first place. I
will take your tiny pinches any day as when you find comfort in
my skin,
it gives it worth.
When it reddens and bruises, it reminds me that it is still mine.

Depths

It's funny how once you've dragged me to your depths you look at me as if you aren't sure how I got there and why I don't just climb out. Forgetting the view from down here isn't the same as it is up there. And you're the one that brought me down.

Kisses

You drop kisses on my skin like the softest rain,
Watering every surface of me,
with more consideration and intention than the skies ever
had.

And when every pore of mine rises to meet you,
Then like the Earth, I know I am loved.

More

When people ask me
as they inevitably do
will I have more, when will it be
as if it is some small feat to have grown a world inside me.
To have given myself over to you as wholey as I did.

I make sure to tell them
about the pains we went through.
How my choices were taken or bent and how those first
moments we had together

were so brief before I had to place you inside a plastic box and
offer up my prayers to Eileithyia.

I lost my voice for a while. They made sure to keep me weak
without sleep and unable to advocate for you.
Don't worry, my flower because I found it again.
I made sure to raise hell for you when you needed it
but in devoting myself to you, l forgot to do so for myself.

Finding that balance is now easier
and I will never love you any less for the trials you will not
remember

but I make sure to tell them. That in asking if I want more
they are telling me and you and any other woman that what I
did was easy.

Easy and expected.

I may do, I may not. But that is none of your business.
And the last thing you should tell a woman is that she is not
enough.

Passion

Sometimes I feel like we've traded passion for contentment and
then there are those stolen moments
where I grip your skin and they slip slightly from the heat of us
and I tell you to go slow so your kisses burn,
so I ache almost painfully,
before you've really touched me
and just a graze of your fingers across my shoulder blade and
your teeth at my neck causes me to abandon reason.
And I know contentment isn't the opposite of passion.

Disclaimer

You are a walking disclaimer. Always preparing people for the worst, to meet you as you are.
When really you need no introduction.

Bruises

I used to wonder how she dealt with his ferocity.
Before realising the kidnap was a lie, because how could she
find something redeemable in such a king? Then I wondered
how she tamed him.
How he was soft for her and no one else.
And this is something I thought would fill my hunger;
to be the one you are soft for which only led to bowing at the
feet of lesser gods and getting trampled.

But I've come to realise how Persephone and I differ is that I
need a mate
who is unassuming for others but solid and unbending for me. So
maybe they wonder who you are behind your quiet and
diplomacy,

but while these are admirable qualities I always knew
that there was more to you than that and it burns me up in
times I'm able to remember the things you can do to me.

It's a bit warmer today and I'm wearing shorts that creep up my
thighs that stick to the leather seats on the way
to work and real life.
And as I sit I see the fingermarks,

the soft bruises you left on me last night,
trailing my skin, disappearing under the seams.
And I can't say I'm mad as I remember
all the ways you weren't gentle with me as you devoted
yourself in service to me for the hours we had.
Those moments we take where we don't have to play the roles
don't have to be the king and queen but wear our crowns all
the same.

I wonder if anyone else notices the purple lines of power you
have imprinted on me as I move about my day.
Perhaps they don't care but I can't help but smile as I think
they do.

Rest & Pleasure

I find myself pulling in. My body craving a rest so full I am unable to deliver. No matter how many early nights, I am always in debt to my body and further in debt to my mind that seeks the kneading and stretching that work and sleep and TV and tasteless food cannot provide. I lose it. My mind, that is, in a book of others doing things I am unable to do. And I don't want to be this person, just existing. I want to thrive. I want to rule this kingdom of mine as myself. Not this shell that just gets by, just exists. I want to fall into hedonism like a vat of cream, enveloping me and clinging to me until I am dripping with pleasure. I guess that's what I thought the underworld was all about.

Persephone

The woman

Before I'm Ready

I should always go home before I'm not ready. I wish I would learn my lesson. At 30 years old I still do this any chance I get. I push the night beyond its breaking point to the moment I realise I should have left before. When I wasn't ready. When I still had a chance to say it was a great night, I wanted more. But I don't. I get greedy and selfish and hoard the enjoyment like it will never come along again and I end the night wishing that I went home before I was ready.

And I go back to nothing good ever happens after 2am. And it does I say. That time I say. But when was the last time I got to 2am unaided, unsubstituted, unabashed. When was the last time I left after 2am and hadn't wished I had gone home already?

I'm ashamed. I'm embarrassed and I'm scared I've done something I said I would never do and would never do again. And I am irrevocably broken when I don't need to be.

You slept in our warm bed with my pyjamas next to you all night. As if you were waiting for me to lift the covers and join you. Crawl under the duvet at 10 or 11 or 12 or 1 but instead I creep home at gone 6 and the Uber driver asks me if I'm on my way to work and I say "*no, home.*"

I make myself promises of how this will go next time and some I think I will keep but others I probably won't and I remind myself of all the bad things and the nothing things and the anything but good things that happens after 2am and I listen to you play downstairs whilst I try to erase my night and hope I can come to you as a better me when I wake.

Amends

And in my dreams, we've made amends,
You tell me you've forgiven and introduce me to your newest life and love,
And suddenly we are almost as important to each other as we were before,
We start to knit together but the gaps remain and
Maybe our pieces don't fit together as they did.

Because this story wasn't meant to end in redemption,
And reconciliation.
It was just our time to part.
Our time to draw our roots away and give us both a chance to grow,
Deeper into the earth.

Back to Spring

Was this how Persephone felt when she returned to spring? Six months cultivating an empire, feeling firmer on her feet and finally able to spread her vines without fear only to descend into true darkness the moment the seasons change.

I thought I had put this all behind me. I was so sure
I had finally grown into myself.
Take me or leave me this was who I was born to be.
But something seems to have been lost in transition. The things I never thought I would be again. Afraid, insecure, embarrassed of myself. I wasn't that girl any more.
But here I am and I hate how small it makes me feel.
How I pull back my stems and watch them wither at the ends.

Maybe I just have to wait out the spring and I will be queen again when this season is over but there's every chance I will forever be afraid of returning to spring.

I Am

I am calm, I am capable
I am loved and I matter
I am calm, I am capable
I am loved and I matter
I am calm, I am capable
I am loved and I matter
I am calm, I am capable
I am loved and I matter
I am calm, I am capable
I am loved and I matter
I am calm, I am capable
I am loved and I matter
I am calm, I am capable
I am loved and I matter
I am calm, I am capable
I am loved and I matter
I am calm, I am capable
I am loved and I matter
I am calm, I am capable
I am loved and I matter

Choice

I've heard people say if you fall in love with two people, choose the second because if you loved the first person, you wouldn't have fallen in love with the second, but I don't believe that. Love is both out of our hands and a choice.

No one person fills every gap, so sometimes without trying, your heart finds someone who ticks the boxes that your lover can't, and while that may be a failing of monogamy, no one will tick the same boxes you do or bring boxes like gifts I didn't know I wanted.

You are not the one I stay with because I made a choice one day that I am beholden to like pomegranate seeds. You are the one I choose every day. Our life together is the life I choose. In every decision, my choice is you.

Love Potion

I wish I could bottle every nice word that anybody has ever said about me. I'd keep a lid on it most days but some days I would pour it out into a glass and drink the words like an elixir and remedy my ills. My very own love potion.

You are a good listener
You are thoughtful
You are funny
You are kind
You tell the best stories
You look beautiful

New

I think it's hard to accept that you will never be you again.
Or you will – but not the you that you remember. Not the you
you're thinking of.
You've shed that skin,
and that's OK because this fresh new skin underneath whole
pink and soft is you.

The you that you are now.

I expect that's why I find I can't forgive people. Those people
who ripped some of my skin from me. The ones who force me
to grow fresh skin over the wounds and heal myself. Because it
means I have to let go of the me that I knew. And this new me is
that much softer for a while. But eventually I'll be so calloused
and scarred I won't know the version of myself I used to be, and
where she went, or if any of her remains.

That's why I tether myself in my relationships, as I left part of
her with everyone I knew and just like you can take something
away I can give it too and maybe that means one day I'll get her
back.

Just as someone new.

River

I take my anxiety down to the river,
Intending to wash it away and out to sea, but the water is stagnant and full to the banks,
With others who have done the same,
But not managed to let go,
I drop to me knees on the grassy shore and claw at the earth, gazing deeply
Into the mother who never gave this pain for me,
Nor deserves me tearing grass from her scalp this way.
I bury it down deep inside the earth and watch it beat there from my window,
Like the tell-tale heart, mocking me for moving on.

Afraid

I'm afraid.
I'm afraid of ageing.
I'm afraid of not being beautiful any more,
Of becoming invisible,
Because I'll disappear if not observed.

I hate it.
I hate that I'm afraid,
For all the reasons I shouldn't be,
For all the reasons I tell others not to be,
For all the things I am that aren't my face.

I'm afraid.
I'm afraid I will lose
my semblance of power over men,
Because we all know that in this world,
we have so little.

I'm ashamed of how much space it takes up,
Of how much of myself I devoted to fixing and preserving,
When I report to love myself so much,
Because how can I only love one version of me?

Love is not so shallow.

And I feel most sad when I watch her
look in the mirror and smile,
And pose for photos however she likes,
And be herself in everything she does,
without consideration for how she looks.

And it pains me.
It pains me that one day,
she might not feel that way,
and worse still that she might not feel that way,
because of how I chose to be,

How I chose to be afraid.

Growth is a Graveyard

I want to leave myself. If just for a little while but growth is a graveyard, so I shed myself like a soul leaves its shell, every time I want to leave who I am for a while.
For in leaving myself, I discover the strengths and frailties, buried and new.

Growth is a graveyard, a cycle, a path intertwined, filled with layers of self-hate and self-doubt and secrets about myself I never knew.

So, I leave myself, but not in surrender,
I evolve, I learn, I grow, I remember.
As I free myself from this skin and moths fly from my ribcage I shed who I am,
Only to discover a strong soul still resides. I can redress it again and again but no matter what, I will never leave myself behind. Because growth is a graveyard and in the graveyard, I am home.

Love Is

He brings me a drink before bed, because he knows I will be thirsty.
He does drop off in the mornings, because he knows I need extra time in bed.

She clasps my face in her hands, because she wants to look into my eyes.
I laugh at the small things she does, because it's so adorable my heart bursts with joy.
She asks me to sing even though I'm terrible at it, because it soothes her.

She curls up with me, because she knows I'm in pain.

She hug me (even though it feels like hugging an ironing board), because she doesn't see me often any more.

He brags about me to his friends, because he is proud of me.

She cares for my child like her own, because she can.

She messages me "oi" because I didn't answer, because she knows sometimes I just need a kick.

Love is all this and more. Love is what lives in this house.

The Story of Us

I've grow with you,
In all directions,
From (not quite) maiden,
To goddess (still in practice),
With no trickery involved.

And while from the outside,
It looks like we took a straight path,
(I really was so young when we met), But
it gave us more time,
For our beings to entangle like mint.

And those perched on clouded mountains,
Look down at us and say,
I can bend you to my will with brass vines,
But we know that if you bend,
It's of your own accord.

You never showed me my power,
But gave me space to find it,
And keep finding it, myself
and I don't doubt that,
I helped to water you too.

Our roots are deep,
Our bones are strong,
Our thrones are gold,
And I know that while we may not be immortal,
Our love still climbs.
We've planted seeds to help them grow.

Thank you so much for reading.

Please leave a review on Amazon or Goodreads so more people can find this book.

About the Author

Laura Barber works in marketing but spends most of her free time chasing her toddler and trying to squeeze writing into any time left over. She is a proud feminist and is passionate about highlighting bi-erasure, everyday racism and encouraging self-love. Living the chaotic dream with husband Nic, her daughter Alba, and their three-legged Frenchie Luna. When not juggling office life and home life, she's penning essays and poetry—fuelled by copious amounts of vegan doughnuts.

You can connect with me on:

🌐 laurabarberauthor.com

g goodreads.com/lozbarber93

[f] laurabarberauthor

◎ lozbarber93

Also by Laura Barber

Just Between Friends

Perfect for fans of Sally Rooney's Normal People and David Nicholls' One Day. Just Between Friends is a seductive read about friendship and love and the inherent messiness that comes with being human.

Printed in Great Britain
by Amazon

44363078R00046

Printed in Great Britain
by Amazon